His Doctor at Sea

Fiona McArthur

Prologue

D r Kiri Fender gazed hard across the blue of the Mediterranean to the distant houses. They clung like pastel limpets onto the cliffs of Italy and as they blurred, and she closed her eyes to stave off the memories until she could breathe in the beauty in front of her.

Gratitude. Not something she'd done when she'd first boarded the ship, but it was easier now as she listened to the delight of the newly embarked passengers.

These first few hours sailing along the Italian coast were her favorite times, but duty called, so she brushed the hair out of her eyes and turned towards the hospital below. Four months of shipboard routines had brought the purpose back into her life and she was so grateful for that.

Her smile slipped. It was only five days until "the anniversary of that day" would be behind her and then everything would be easier.

Chapter 1: Stefano

P rince Stefano Adolphi Phillipe Augustus Mykonides tried not to think of the worst-case scenario as he rolled the unconscious wife of his brother into the recovery position. With immense relief he noted the blue of her lips improve slightly as her airway cleared.

He'd hoped Theros could stay out of trouble on his wife's birthday holiday but it seemed it wasn't so. With a sigh, the eldest son of Prince Paulo of Aspelicus, a tiny but wealthy principality in the Mediterranean Sea, couldn't help the familiar guilt that his brother had done something else chronically stupid.

'Get the ship's hospital on the phone,' Stefano said with bitter control. Glancing up at Theros, his brother stood helpless as ever, his handsome face, so like his own, twisted in distress. 'Tell them it's an emergency.'

Theros's mouth worked silently, like the child he was, and he swayed, shocked and incredulous as his wife began to turn blue again.

Stefano hardened his voice to a stern order. 'Theros. Now! Tell them it's a reaction to latex. To bring adrenalin.' He said the words slowly and enunciated clearly.

Theros blinked and stumbled to the phone as Stefano began to strip Marla of her skin-tight rubber playsuit, cursing under his breath as her breathing became more laboured. A small voice in his head murmured; be thankful that at least Theros had had the good sense to call him in time.

He needed to remove the offending clothing as fast as possible — hopefully before his sister-in-law stopped breathing. Not an easy job, which he gathered should have been half the fun. What he would have given for a scalpel...

Chapter 2: Kiri

Ten doors away Dr Kiri Fender jogged down the gold and blue carpet of the passageway leading to the largest suites, running over in her head what she knew about latex allergies. In truth Kiri was the on-call doctor for crew, not passengers, and she hoped her boss would follow quickly in case the patient was *in extremis*.

She'd hate to lose a patient on departure day, and a royal personage at that would be very poor form. Terrible luck that Will had been on a cabin visit when the call came in, so she was it, for now at least.

She didn't even bother to imagine the cause of this latex exposure. She'd tossed the usual personal protection gloves out from the emergency pack and donned latex-free ones, reminding herself they should use them in the whole medical center in this current climate of escalating allergies, and had packed extra adrenalin ampoules. In her hand she carried a box with the Epi-Pen inside which made administration much quicker in such emergencies.

She prayed the patient's airways wouldn't have closed completely by the time her boss arrived with extra help.

When the door opened, she barely glanced at the distressed man in black shiny underwear and focused ahead to the woman on the floor. Another man was bent over her as he struggled to extricate her legs from skin-tight rubbery leggings.

There was something oddly familiar about the shape of his head, the shoulders, the powerful biceps, but she shut that thought down, her attention on the patient who appeared unconscious. Her skin had blotched with a paling red rash.

Kiri spoke to the dark hair of the man kneeling on the carpet as she bent down beside him. 'Is she breathing?'

'Just.'

Kiri glanced at the man's face and recognition slapped her like one of the white-capped waves slapped the hull of the ship.

What the hell was Stefano Mykonides doing on her ship?

Lock that away, quick-smart, she chastised herself, as she unboxed the Epi-Pen and pinched the woman's leg to inject the adrenalin. Her gaze skimmed the almost naked woman for any change in the tiny rapid rises of her chest. Those movements would tell if the medication was helping. Most times with this type of shock, recovery would be dramatic as the drug turned off the body's flooding allergic response like a tap.

But a tiny section of her brain still tried to work out what on earth was going on? The Stefano she'd known... well this didn't seem his style.

She heard her boss and the nurse arrive with the emergency stretcher as Stefano leaned towards her.

His steel grey eyes boring into hers, Stefano murmured, 'We expect you to remain discreet about this event.'

A pulse beat visibly in his strong neck and a part of her responded in the wrong way — the most inappropriate of ways – and that increased her dislike. She met his eyes and tried, though she doubted with much success, to keep the contempt from her face. So typical. This woman was fighting for her life, yet Stefano was all about the good name of the Mykonides family.

She could say a few things about his good name. Instead, she bit out an ultra polite, 'Of course, Your Highness.' But the look she sent him could have scooped up the scorn with a spoon.

Stefano turned back to extricating Marla's foot.

Thankfully, before she said something she would regret, Marla groaned and stirred, and Kiri heard his sigh of relief as she leant over and spoke near the patient's ear. 'You're okay. Take it easy.'

She looked at him and silently mouthed '*Name?*' as the last of the trouser leg came free with an elastic snapping *thwang*.

'Marla. Mykonides. My brother's wife.' Out of the corner of her eye she saw him slide the rubber suit under the seat of the lounge chair out of sight as more medical staff approached.

Kiri rolled her eyes at his priorities as she turned back to her patient. 'I'm going to put another needle — a cannula — in your arm and tape it there, Marla, as a precaution, but you're improving every second.'

The cannula slid in easily. Always a relief when a patient was peripherally shut down from shock.

'This is only a precaution,' she said to the dazed woman, 'in case you need further medication or intravenous fluids.' But within herself, Kiri gauged the response adequate from the initial dose — often the way — and it seemed the medical crisis was over. Not the other one though.

She felt the trolley being manoeuvred in beside her and Stefano stood up.

He said, 'Please take my toweling robe,' and handed it to Kiri to cover the patient with.

Her nod of appreciation wasn't only for the gown for Marla, but because with him gone there seemed so much more air around the patient... and herself. More distance. Funny, that, and funny that she wasn't in the mood for laughing.

She'd always had a respiratory-like awareness of him — like her own damned anaphylaxis — but she'd thought herself desensitized against that response after what she'd been through. Later, off-duty and on her own, she'd worry about that.

'Dr Hobson.' Kiri glanced at her boss, the senior ship's doctor as he knelt beside her. 'This is Mrs. Marla Mykonides.'

'Princess Marla,' Stefano corrected, and Kiri closed her eyes briefly to block all the deceit from the past.

'Princess Marla suffered severe unexpected anaphylaxis to latex. We've removed the causative agent.' She flicked an ironic glance at Stefano and the departed leggings before she turned back to her boss.

Dr Wilhelm Hobson leaned over and took the woman's wrist to feel her pulse. 'You've given adrenalin?'

'Two minutes ago.' Kiri finished taping the intravenous cannula in place.

Marla groaned and her eyes stayed open now. Staring. 'Where am I?'

'All is well, madam. You're in your cabin. Your husband and brother-in-law are here. Rest. You'll feel better soon.' She rested her hand over Marla's in sympathy. She and Will looked at the welts on her arms that seemed to be fading before their eyes. 'Good response, as you see.'

Will nodded, then wrote the dose and time down on his scribe sheet while Kiri took the blood pressure cuff from the nurse and wrapped it around Marla's arm while the nurse crouched down to inflate the cuff and listen. Nobody spoke.

'Still some shock,' the nurse said, and reading the number Kiri could see the pressure was very low. As expected.

The nurse began to adhere cardiac dots to the patient's skin and the sound of a racing heartbeat permeated the room. The team assembled the intravenous infusion to increase the pressure in Marla's blood vessels with an extra fluid bolus.

Confident now that their patient was stable, Will stood up and faced the two men in the room.

This'll be good, Kiri thought, and though she didn't look away from her patient her ears were tuned for their explanation.

'And who is responsible for this woman?' Wilhelm's tone rang deadly serious. But then he was serious most of the time. Kiri's attention shifted briefly to Stefano to see his reaction and...

Their eyes met, clashed, and uh-oh. She should not have looked.

Chapter 3: Stefano

Stefano felt in shock himself, much like poor Marla without the benefit of the drug's reversal.

Kiri Fender was *here* and to see her like this... As medic to his family, dynamic, so confident of her skills as he knew she was. But it was not these things he remembered the most, it was the jolt, the instant awareness he always felt when he looked at her. The heat that flared between them. Not the woman who looked at him with distaste and called him Your Highness with undisguised contempt.

He could not dwell on this now. Not now. Like everything in his life, this too, would have to wait.

Stefano had watched Marla's condition improve with immense relief and now he refocused on the wider picture. Kiri, down on the floor with Marla, ignored him as he deserved. He glanced at the man in charge — a stocky blond-headed man with a South African accent and air of command. A ship this size would need a competent senior. One who knew how to be discreet.

Then he looked to Theros. His brother stood, twisting his hands across his body, suddenly perhaps aware that he looked strange in those ridiculous shorts. His mouth worked but, as usual in times of stress, nothing came out.

Stefano sighed and stepped forward. Of course he was responsible. He had been since the moment of Theros's accident all those years ago. Dressed only in swim-trunks, facing the room, he glanced coolly at the medic. 'I am.'

He should not have noticed Kiri flinch as he made that admission, but he did. Had she hoped otherwise? It shouldn't have mattered. Didn't matter. She'd always expected him to be more than he really was, a prince who lied and made promises he didn't keep.

She didn't look his way. 'Okay, Ginger,' she said to the nurse. 'Let's help Princess Marla up onto the trolley and we'll take her down to the hospital for observation.'

Fifteen minutes later Stefano paced in front of the window in his brother's suite. 'Please remove those ridiculous shorts,' he said. Stefano paced very slowly, with rigid control, frustrated at his brother's propensity for disaster and his own for not preventing it, and at the fruitless urge to ask why he had to deal with this.

He knew why.

At seven Stefano had pulled Theros from a deep ocean pool on their island and saved his life with a boy's rough and ready resuscitation that had not been sufficient to prevent damage. Theros had been left with an injury to part of his brain from its time without oxygen.

After that Stefano's young brother had not been the most sensible of boys, and later had become a handsome, impish, immature man who never grew up.

But that had not stopped Theros from diving into mischief and danger whenever he could, and as often as he was able, Stefano would be the one to rescue him.

'Stefano?'

Theros's troubled voice brought him back to the present, and he stared at his brother. 'Trouble. It will find you in the dark. Or in this case broad daylight. Is sex so tedious with your wife that you must risk her life with latex?'

Theros wrung his hands. 'No. *No.* One of her friends gave the suits to us for her birthday. We were playing. Laughing. Suddenly she could not breathe. I did not know Marla would have trouble with the playsuit. The rubber made her not breathe?'

'Latex.' Stefano squeezed the skin under his nose in a pincer grip to stop himself from losing patience. He never lost patience with Theros. Never forgot his father's grief and blame.

He should have been faster in summoning help and perhaps his brother's brain would not have been damaged. This was the legacy of guilt he could not shake.

The job of protecting the family — and Theros in particular — from ridicule had fallen to Stefano, and he had protected his brother well for many years. He was still willing to carry that mantle regardless of the impact on his own life. But it had been a tough year.

His foray into medicine — the vocation that should have been Theros's — had stemmed from that guilt, from his father's distress and disappointment. It had been his own lack of ability to prevent such a sequela for his brother. Even at such a young age he had vowed if such a situation ever arose again he would know what to do. Unexpectedly, medicine had also provided a true vocation, and something that soothed his soul and gave him purpose.

His father, Crown Prince Paulo III of Aspelicus, had hired a sensible woman to supervise Theros while Stefano had been away at a medical symposium in Australia earlier that year, and to everyone's surprise his simple brother had found true love.

At his father's urgent request Stefano had rushed home from the arms of Dr Kiri Fender... but too late.

Theros had already eloped. Then Stefano himself had been involved in a serious motor vehicle accident and during his slow recovery many months had passed.

To his unexpected relief, Theros's sensible wife, Marla, had proved helpful in steering Theros on a more stable path, but even the most sensible could make an unfortunate mistake.

Any notion of Stefano being released from his duty of care was a misconception. Theros would always need him.

Which underlined something he'd always known, he was no catch for the woman of his heart. This was no life to offer a vibrant and intelligent woman like Kiri and that was without even the strictures of royal duty.

In the harsh light of reality he knew that as heir to the throne he should let go of what had passed between he and Dr Fender in Australia. But he should have sent her an explanation instead of silence when he hadn't returned.

Theros coughed and Stefano returned to the present. His brain could not seem to settle without flitting back to Kiri.

His brother's eyes searched for reassurance.

Stefano took his fingers from his face and stared at Theros so he could be sure he was listening, perhaps even absorbing the gravity of the situation.

'Marla could have died. It was close. She almost did.' He paused, let that settle in. 'She must carry an injection, similar to that which the doctor had, in case she is exposed to this product again accidentally.' He stared hard. 'You are her husband and it is your duty to keep her safe. Do you understand?'

'Yes, Stefano.' Theros chewed his lip. 'The doctor said she would be all right, though? They'll let her out of the hospital this afternoon?'

Not surprisingly, Theros had an irrational fear of hospitals, which hadn't been helped when Stefano had nearly died in a recent accident.

Stefano saw that fear and his irritation with his brother seeped further away. His voice gentled. 'For the moment the danger is gone. Yes. If you are careful it will not return.'

Theros peeled his own shiny underwear from his well-endowed body and sadly handed them to Stefano. 'And she will be fine tomorrow, won't she? We're going to Naples to climb Vesuvius. You're coming with us?'

'My leg is stiff. Not this time.' Why must his brother love adventures that required exposure to the public? It was so much easier on their island home off mainland Greece, and he had many things that required his attention there. But his father had asked him to watch over them on this short cruise that Theros had promised his wife.

Ashore, his man could be with them, but none of them had imagined he would need watching in the bedroom. That was bad luck and nobody's fault. Except his.

Tomorrow, while they were touring it would be a good time for he, Stefano, to apologize to Dr Kiri Fender.

Finding Kiri where he least expected her, slightly shattered himself by a response he hadn't expected, he now had pressing matters to attend to. An explanation for his non-return. And a plea for forgiveness. If she would listen.

Kiri, who was not his Kiri, cared little for his consequence.

The problem was that the woman he'd left behind in Australia had stayed like a halo around his heart. He, of all people, knew it wasn't sensible to desire a woman who did not understand the tedious ways of royal commitment. As heir, in his country's crises, *he* was the one who was called and she was the one who was left.

But still he smarted from the thinly veiled contempt in her sea-blue eyes, because he remembered the warmly passionate, fun-loving side of sweet Kiri. The gods must be laughing at this insult to his pride.

If they had been destined to meet again this was not how he would have orchestrated the moment.

Less than an hour ago she'd hated him. Clearly. And that hurt.

She'd always been confident, sassy, and so different from the women he knew. Of course he'd been recklessly drawn to the young doctor who challenged and laughed with him during his Sydney study tour. What a week *that* had been.

He would admit he had not behaved thoughtfully during their intense time together. Everything had progressed far too quickly. They'd immersed themselves in each other for a torrid affair of incredible closeness, tucked away from the world in her tiny flat when they weren't at the hospital.

Tomorrow he would finish this. Seek her forgiveness, allow himself to let go, and then he would marry as his father wished to secure the succession and fulfil his destiny. But for the moment his man-boy brother needed reassurance.

Theros was playing with the legs of the latex suit he'd found under the chair and Stefano reached out and took them from him gently. 'Manos will drive you to Vesuvius.'

'Oh, good. And Marla will come.'

'Yes. If she is up to it.'

Theros looked childishly happy and Stefano supposed it was good that *someone* was pleased.

Theros went to find food, accompanied by Manos, and Stefano returned to his own cabin. Until another crisis created by his brother required his immediate presence. Like the night he had left Kiri's bed and flown out intending to return and explain why the future was not theirs to plan.

Even that had not worked out when he'd been involved in an accident that left him recovering for months of rehabilitation. Almost losing his leg, he'd barely been able to look at himself in the mirror, let alone consider showing himself to a woman.

But that excuse had gone now, except for the jagged and extensive scarring behind knee and thigh, he was almost well. Now his treatment of Kiri Fender made him feel ashamed despite the fact he had tried. It was another burden of guilt he found he could not move on from, because it had taken him almost five months before he was able to rule his own life again. A loss of control he never wanted to experience again.

By the time he had begun to search for her, at least to attempt an explanation, she'd been untraceable.

At first he had tried the hospital in Sydney, then her home phone, mail to her old lodgings. He did not know her friends or family. She had disappeared without a trace. It seemed, ironically, to this very ship.

Chapter 4: Kiri

Four hours later, in the ship's medical center ten floors below the royal suite, Dr Hobson was ready to discharge the Princess... the one who just wanted to be called Marla.

'You can go back to your rooms.' Kiri helped her dress in the clothes that had been sent down for her. 'Your rash is gone and observations are all normal now. They should remain that way if you stay free of exposure to latex.'

Poor Marla blushed again. 'No more birthday gifts that almost end it all!'

Kiri grimaced with her. 'It was bad luck.' There was a lot of that around at the moment, my word there was, Kiri thought, aggrieved at fate. 'Allergies can be to anything and build unexpectedly. It could have been something as simple as peanuts.'

'Except there's nothing embarrassing about peanuts.' Marla sighed. 'I'm supposed to be the sensible one. But thanks for that.'

'Hey, it was your birthday and you got a fun gift.' Kiri shrugged. 'At least now you know latex sets up a reaction in your body. You can make sure if you ever go into hospital the staff keep you latex-free.'

The young woman nodded and stared down at the little Epi-Pen in her hand.

'And be careful with that.' Kiri nodded at the pen. 'You can get into trouble if you inject it in the wrong place.'

'True,' Will offered helpfully. 'I saw a man once who injected it into his thumb trying to work the plunger. It's a powerful drug and it shuts down the peripheral blood flow. His thumb had to be removed for gangrene.'

Kiri flashed a look at her boss before she helped Marla up. 'Imagine what a disgruntled wife could do?'

The senior medic held out his hands in horror with a side-serve of reproach. 'Don't go there, Kiri!'

She shook her head in amusement, because Wilhelm's seriousness always cracked her up. 'Is he scaring you, Marla?'

'Only because of my darling husband. He is trouble with a capital T.' The girl laughed and shook her head. 'I will not let Theros near it. I truly can be sensible.'

a

She could see that. Everyone in the clinic had come to that conclusion despite the circumstances under which they'd met. 'Not too sensible.' Kiri smiled. 'You should still enjoy your birthday. It's such a shame this has marred your holiday.' She couldn't help thinking that Marla wasn't the only one whose voyage had been affected. And this week of all weeks, when her emotions were already on rollercoaster alert. Bummer. Bummer. *Bummer.*

Usually fair-minded, Kiri guessed she owed Stefano an apology for the faces she'd pulled... but it wasn't going to happen. She still didn't get why he was on his brother's holiday as his minder — on *her* ship — the guy was a prince, didn't he have his own luxury liner? But most of all, it was hard to forget that somewhere above her head was the man she'd accepted she'd never see again.

She glanced up. Up there, larger than life and twice as disconcerting — because she'd lost her common sense in the sensual haze they'd created together.

Ginger's offer to escort Marla to the suite was jumped on with enthusiasm: no way was Kiri going back up there. Self-preservation wins every time now. During the long weeks while she'd waited for his promised return, during the phone calls when she'd tried to contact him, emails asking for him to reply so she could speak to him, it had been a wake-up call she hadn't expected. Not after the time they'd spent together.

That had been an unexpected blow to her usual resilience when he hadn't replied, and she'd been so sick and weak, barely able to function in early pregnancy, that she hadn't been able to motivate herself to do anything more about it.

By the time the first nausea-filled trimester had passed and she'd begun to feel more like herself again, Kiri had accepted that Stefano wasn't coming back. He had clearly decided his royal status meant she'd been forgotten.

Well, she and her baby didn't need him.

All her life she'd been independent, the youngest sister to three brilliant sisters much older than her, with her doctor parents always busy. The only person she'd felt connected to had been her big brother Nick. And briefly Stefano.

But the thought of a baby of her own, to love and nurture, to be loved in return. A team of two. The prospect had excited and centered her.

Until eighteen weeks... A time when she'd already begun to create a nursery of tiny clothes, whimsical toys, and softest wraps, the pains had come and suddenly her baby was gone.

In a matter of days it would be her baby's due date. It would pass and she would finally be able to move on. She'd promised herself.

The best thing she'd done for herself was taking her brother's suggestion to come here and move on to a new life.

Wilhelm wandered back into the main office. 'Marla seems very sweet.'

'She does.' Kiri blinked and came back to the present.

'Embarrassing for our royal guests, though.' Will raised his brows as he waved Ginger off duty on her return and shut the clinic door.

'Mortifying.' Kiri said with a little too much relish. 'I bet her brother-in-law hated that!'

Even in the brief time they'd been together, Stefano's avoidance of the whole topic of his royalty and his absolute disgust with the press had been obvious. At the time it had seemed sensible — she knew little of the life of a very minor royal, which was the impression of himself he'd projected. Not that she'd even thought about it much when they were together. As her man he'd been able to help her forget the world. To forget herself.

She dragged her mind back to Marla and Theros.

'It's Marla's birthday. They've been married less than a year. And Theros wanted to holiday on a cruise ship instead of their island like most of the family do.'

Will shrugged. 'So why is his brother here? Heir to the throne, the most famous reconstructive surgeon in the Med and all that. A bit high-powered for a minder, don't you think?'

So Will had picked up on Stefano's medical fame, too. Kiri tried for a careless shrug. 'Family name is very important to everyone, so I imagine in a royal family it would be more so.' She wasn't sure who she was trying to convince, Will or herself. 'Apparently Marla's husband has bad luck with the press.'

Kiri picked up her bag, but he put his hand up to stop her. 'One sec.'

She paused, looked back, and her stomach sank. She'd hoped nothing had been noticed. Nothing had been said. She hadn't even looked at Stefano again as they'd wheeled Marla out.

He scratched his brow thoughtfully. 'So? What's going on between you two?'

'Which two?' She switched off a computer she'd thankfully missed at shutdown. An excuse to turn away.

Will waited patiently and Kiri felt the blush heat her cheeks. The silence stretched and she didn't like silence. That was her only excuse for being unable to extricate herself. 'You mean Stefano Mykonides?' How the heck had Will sensed that? 'I don't know what you mean. There's nothing going on with us.'

But the flood of memories she'd been holding back all day rose like a wave in her throat. Such rotten timing. She concentrated on her feet, on planting them firmly on the deck. She was *not* going under.

Control re-established, she turned back to Will.

He tilted his head and went on. 'Come on, Kiri. I may be a tad oblivious at times but the air was thick between you two and our Prince was watching your neck like Dracula on a diet. Nick didn't mention you knew any Mediterranean royalty.'

Because she'd told no one about her stupidity — not even her brother, and definitely not any of her sisters. 'Nick has nothing to do with this.' Because her brother Nick would be out for Stefano's blood if he knew what the Prince had done to his little sister. 'Stefano is a surgical consultant. I worked with him briefly in Sydney during my last rotation.'

'You worked with Mykonides?'

Will looked even more interested, not less, and Kiri could feel the walls of the little clinic begin to close in on her. She didn't want to think about that time with Stefano, let alone talk about it, but her South African colleague could miss the obvious sometimes.

He proved it. 'So? What happened? Spill.'

'That's all there is.' To her horror her eyes filled with tears. Not because of Stefano or Will's insistence that she share, but at the thought of the sadness that had been building for this past week.

Will blinked, his face changing as he recognized her distress. 'Hey, I've upset you. So sorry. I just want you to know I'm here to listen if you need an ear.' He raised his hands in defense. 'I promised Nick I'd look out for you.'

Don't mention this to Nick. But if she said it out loud it would be the first thing he'd do. 'I'm a big girl, Will. I don't want to talk about it. Don't need to talk about it.' Even she could hear the over-reaction. She sighed.

Too vehement.

She turned away to wipe at the tear that had slid out against her will. 'Sorry. Water under the bridge, that's all.'

'Well, if he gives you a hard time, just let me know,' Will said gruffly, but she didn't reply. She nodded once and fled.

When Kiri finally fell asleep that night her dreams were filled with the sensation of being lost and alone, and always in the distance was Stefano, turned the other way and choosing not to see her.

When she woke she had tears on her cheeks, and despite the sun streaming in she was so exhausted she wanted to roll over and bury her head. Her shift didn't start until eleven but she wouldn't get back to sleep. Through the open window she could hear the mooring crew as they secured the ship to the wharf in Naples, and she lay on her bunk and felt the ship creak and strain against its ropes.

And that made her think of yesterday's latex session gone wrong.

Unwillingly, she felt her lips curve — which wasn't a bad thing considering the night — and she knew at some stage she would have to share the story — names changed to protect the innocent — with her closest sibling. Nick would certainly enjoy the sense of the ridiculous.

She still didn't get why Stefano was on his brother's holiday.

From the brief mention Stefano had made of Aspelicus, Kiri gathered the island was a beautiful cliff-edged principality with a harbor originally on the trade routes as a safe haven. An island once home to an ancient Greek school of physicians, now with a splinter school on the more southern island of Asclepius.

She'd spent hours online and discovered it had grown more Italian and French since its Greek heritage, and that its royal family were far more famous than she'd realized.

She'd been a fool. Of *course* Stefano had not returned for a brief fling he'd once had in the Antipodes. His family had developed a stronghold in spices and teas from China, and the tiny monarchy had become incredibly wealthy. More recently it thrived on the sale of gourmet olive oil from the trees that dotted the hills, its cash flow supplemented by high-roller casinos and its own world-famous horse race along the lines of neighboring Monaco's, and a borrowed idea from its neighbor to become a tax haven for residents.

On the other side of the island, a sprawling low-rise hospital had gained international recognition for reconstructive surgery, with Stefano as its director.

The royal family could be traced back a thousand years, but each generation held a physician who had been available for the poorer people as well as those who could pay. It had all read so incredibly romantic and nothing like the few facts Stefano had shared with her.

So she had waited for him to return. But he hadn't.

She could remember as if it were yesterday when she'd applied for the job on the *Sea Goddess,* her brother's old ship. Kiri had always idolized her gorgeous, crazy showman of a big brother — the only one of her high-achieving siblings who understood her.

She never had found out what had precipitated Nick's escape from reality, but for herself it was wanting something totally different from the empty nursery she'd created for a child that would never come. She'd never discussed her loss with anyone — probably foolish and a factor in her slowness to recover — but unable to share with the absent Stefano, she left medicine and chose silence, slipping into the kitchen of a friend's restaurant for a change of lifestyle.

Unlike her older sisters, Nick had seen she wasn't herself and cheered her on. Eventually, with Nick's encouragement, she'd started on the hospitality side of the ship, which had forced her to return to her usual outgoing self, the person she'd lost for a while, and she'd even started to forgive the male of the species, to laugh with Nick's friends and the waiters.

Until she'd begun to miss medicine.

When the opportunity had come, she'd switched roles, and the last three months had been good under Wilhelm's guidance in the ship's hospital.

It had all been fine — *until now.* Who would have thought an ordinary cruise ship would find Stefano and reopen wounds?

Maybe it was time to head home. Hiding from the world had proved fruitless. But why couldn't this have happened next week, when she just knew she'd be stronger? She sighed at the cruelty of timing.

Stefano was here and there was nothing she could do about that. It was time to move on. She'd go and see Will and ask how hard it would be for her to be replaced.

With that thought crystallizing in her mind, Kiri rose from her bed and walked to the window with new purpose. She'd put her notice in and leave as soon as they found someone to take her place.

There were still the next four nights to get through, but she'd manage that once she had a plan in place. She'd foolishly succumbed to ridiculous attraction last time he'd entered her orbit and that would not happen again. Step one was avoiding the Mykonides family. How hard could that be?

Chapter 5: Stefano

Stefano woke with purpose. Today he would deal with what he should have dealt with months ago. Laying this admittedly delectable ghost to rest was well overdue.

He'd discovered the opening times of the ship's hospital, and by the time Theros and Marla had left for their shore-trip the clinic was almost due to close, which suited him perfectly.

He descended the stairs almost at a jog — foolish when his hip would kill him later — and he reminded himself it was not fitting to appear too eager.

The nurse greeted him with a smile. She was the same one he'd seen yesterday, and he inclined his head at the obvious approval he read in her face.

A handsome woman, of the type he'd used to dally with a lifetime ago, she did not interest him now. He had discovered, no matter where he went, Kiri had dampened any desire on his part to consort with other women.

'I wish to see Dr Fender. I am Stefano Mykonides.'

'Of course, Your Highness. I know who you are.'

She smiled at him and blushed. Stefano smiled back blandly, curbing his impatience as the woman went on.

'Dr Fender isn't on duty until later this morning. Perhaps I could help you?'

'No, thank you.'

A door across the waiting room opened and the senior doctor ushered his patient out. As the young boy and his mother walked past them the nurse asked, 'Perhaps Dr Hobson?'

'No.' Stefano inclined his head at the doctor, but before he could leave Hobson crossed the room and held out his hand. They shook hands briefly.

'Ah, Your Highness. Good morning.' He turned to the nurse. 'Can you run those blood samples up to the courier, please?'

He turned back to Stefano. 'I hope all is well with your sister-in-law this morning?'

Stefano tried not to show his irritation, but he was trapped. And where was his quarry if not here? 'Yes. Thank you.' He was over discussing Theros's disasters.

Hobson glanced at his watch. 'How can we help you?'

Stefano inclined his head at the clinic. 'I had hoped to thank Dr Fender, personally, for her timely assistance yesterday. I did not have the opportunity at the time, of course.'

'Of course.'

Hobson smiled non-committally and Stefano quelled the urge to grind his teeth.

'I could convey your appreciation?'

Very pointed, Stefano thought, but he held his temper. 'Thank you, but I wish to do so myself. I will return at another time.'

Hobson didn't shift. 'I'll let her know.'

Stefano could see that the good doctor had assumed protection mode for Kiri. He wondered just what kind of personal relationship he had with his Kiri and had to admit he disliked the idea very strongly. His hand tightened on the room card in his pocket. The card bent. Disliked very strongly. He examined the doctor more closely. He was a well-muscled man, almost as tall as himself, and no doubt attractive to women.

He tested the water. 'Or I could surprise her.'

Robson's smile froze on his face. 'I think she has had enough surprises.'

Stefano had to give the man respect. Loyalty was a good thing, and despite his own misgivings he could not begrudge Kiri her friend's championship. Though his cousin, who owed Stefano many favors, *did* own this shipping line.

His fingers loosened. *Relax. Let it go.* He, too, cared that Kiri was not upset. 'It is not my intention to distress her.'

Hobson met his gaze head-on. 'Good.'

Enough. His day had soured and the pain in his hip from his reckless descent down the stairs was annoying him. 'And good day to you, Dr Hobson.'

Stefano pressed the button for the lift with remarkable restraint, not stupid enough to brave an ascent of twelve floors despite his sudden frustrated desire for explosive energy. The lift doors opened and, as if conjured, Kiri stood waiting to alight.

'Just the person.' Wonderful how good humor could be instantly restored. 'One moment, please, Dr Fender.'

He could not believe his good luck — finally — and gestured for her to wait. With a relief he was careful not to show, he stepped in beside her as she hesitated.

Chapter 6: Kiri

Kiri couldn't believe her bad luck. So close to being safe. 'What if I was on my way to work?'

He shrugged those shoulders that still made her weak at the knees. Damn him. It was so hard not to stare and just remember.

'I have been told you are not working for a few hours.'

Was there a scientific reason his voice made her mouth dry? She searched a little desperately for distraction as she watched him press the lift button for the sixteenth floor.

Of course, he had looked for her in the hospital. If only she hadn't run down for a quick chat with Will.

The doors began to close and for a moment she did consider diving out before they shut – like some female secret agent with a barrel roll in her repertoire — but she'd just look awkward, and probably get sandwiched by the doors.

Or, a hundred times worse, he'd put out his hand and touch her, and she wanted to avoid that at all costs. That was what had happened the first time. He'd laid his hand on her arm to help her from the car and she'd woken up in bed with him. And stayed there for a week.

That left the smart mouth as her only defense. 'So where are we going?' As if she didn't know.

He didn't reply, and she remembered that. The frustrating habits of a man used to answering questions he felt inclined to and ignoring the rest. A prince with his own agenda unless it was for his family. Lucky him. Unlucky her.

She stared straight ahead at the doors of the lift as if they'd magically open and she could float out to safety somewhere in the stairwell. She could feel his eyes on her.

'Why are you on this ship anyway, Your Highness?'

She heard him sigh. 'Do you call me that to annoy me?'

Now she glanced at him. Sugared her voice. 'Is it working?'

He looked at her from under his own raised brows, and then in the ultimate retaliation he smiled. Warm, genuine, gentle even. Blinded, she felt the gesture rip open the wound she'd healed so diligently over the last months aboard ship.

Blast, blast, and double blast. She needed to get away.

She'd fallen in lust with him the first time she'd seen him. Only lust. Please not love. Love wouldn't have ended as it had.

Stefano had smiled at her then, as if they shared a secret, when she'd been late for her last surgical day in the operating theatres because of car trouble. He'd been a guest consultant of her boss and should have reprimanded her like all the other consultants would have done, but instead he'd shown her surgical techniques she'd never thought to witness.

Later, he'd bought her coffee, plied her with cake to replace her missed breakfast, and invited her to ride home with him at the end of the day. When his hand had touched hers, well she'd been hooked, stunned like a landed fish, all big glassy eyes and floppy with desire.

And she knew where that had led.

The flicker of the number lights speeding upwards brought her back to the present and her sense of impending danger grew exponentially. This wasn't sensible. Or safe. Though she wasn't sure whom she was more afraid of. Him or herself.

'I don't want to go anywhere with you.' The words flew out of her mouth and ricocheted around the elevator like silver bullets.

She thought for a moment she'd actually hurt him. There was just a flicker behind his eyes, but that was a joke. Instead he sighed as if she were a troublesome child... or probably just a troublesome subject.

'I will not keep you long.'

Her brows lifted. 'Well, I know *that.*'

This time he did flinch. She saw it. Good, he felt guilty, even though he didn't know how guilty he *should* feel. But she was tired of scoring points and second-guessing his intentions. She just wanted to forget she'd seen him again and re-grow the scar tissue so she could complete her healing.

When the lift stopped she planted her feet more solidly on the spot. He waited for her to pass him and when she didn't he actually lifted his hand to direct her.

She stepped out of his way and back against the wall so fast his hand fell. 'No.' She licked dry lips. 'Goodbye, Prince Stefano. Have a good life.'

There. She'd said it. What she hadn't had a chance to say nine months ago. Now it was done. Finished.

Except he didn't get out, and the silence lengthened.

Without direction from them the lift doors shut and the chamber began its descent to another level.

His voice, when he spoke, remained mild. Slightly amused. 'So, are we to ride up and down in the lift all day until you wish to get out?'

She stepped further to the left of him. 'Leave me alone, Stefano.'

He didn't lift his hand again, but his voice reached out to her. 'Is a few minutes of your time so much to ask? A chance to apologize, explain a little, and then we may part as friends... or less, if that is what you wish.'

She tried to imagine a soft ball of cotton wool jamming her ears to mute the sound. It didn't work. She didn't know how much more of this power struggle she could take before those damn tears she could feel prickling behind her eyes made their escape.

She could get out on another floor, stride away, and then spend the day dreading what could be over in a few minutes if she just faced it. Over and done with. Great theory, but what if it wasn't?

She still wasn't sure whom she trusted least.

The silence lengthened. The lift stopped and began to go down further. 'For goodness' sake. Must you get your own way in everything?'

When he didn't reply, she stepped forward and stabbed the light for the sixteenth floor. The little button rattled with the force. The lift whooshed upwards again.

'Let's get it over with then, shall we?'

Chapter 7: Stefano

Stefano winced. This was not how he had expected it would turn out. A polite thank you, a question as to whether she was well, an apology because he had had to leave so abruptly the last time they'd been together. And, most importantly, he would see that he was not as attracted to the flesh-and-blood woman as his imagination had assured him.

Then he could move on to his duty.

In fact, to his discomfort, the desire for Kiri back in his arms — and most assuredly in his bed — was growing exponentially stronger by the second. Perhaps he should have stepped out of the lift on his own after all. But how was that going to help his predicament? It wouldn't.

The lift doors opened again at his floor and he extended his arm against the doors to hold them. 'After you.'

'Are you? Not again, I hope,' she muttered, and he had to bite back the smile.

This was the woman who had captured his attention over that long-ago week. With her tiny rebellions that always startled him out of his self-assurance, the rapier wit that amused him with its irreverence, the unpredictability of Kiri with the crazy name and so alluring body.

He was in trouble. But, then again, so was she.

Chapter 8: Kiri

Kiri preceded him into the suite and glanced around. The ocean reached into the room with vistas in every direction through enormous windows. Blue of the ocean, white buildings on distant golden cliffs, all glorious under the cerulean sky. Soft carpet under foot, ornate lamps and gold edged furniture. Very grand. Split level. With Stefano.

She hadn't noticed much yesterday — too many other things had been going on. Like a woman critical with shock. Like Stefano reappearing beside her. Like a hundred memories she didn't want to remember.

She kept her back to him. 'Must be cozy, sharing with a married couple.'

'Their suite is very similar. Next door.' Kiri could hear the smile in his voice.

'And your wife's?'

'No wife.' The lock clicked. 'This is my suite.' Why did she feel there was a subtle emphasis on *my*?

She squared her shoulders and faced him. A head taller than her, his lean body muscle-packed under the silk shirt, and those strong thighs encased in bespoke trousers. He appeared more regal than the man she'd known, less approachable now than even the man in the lift. This *was* his suite. His stage. He owned it.

Why did he have to look so damned amazing? 'Fine. Let's have our little conversation and then I'd like to leave.'

He ignored that. The ignoring thing again. He prowled over to the drinks cabinet. Turned to face her and asked mildly, as if they did this every day, 'Would you like something to drink?'

No, but she wouldn't mind something in her hand she could fiddle with — or throw in defense.

Kiri circled the plush sofa and sat on an upright armchair. 'Thank you. Soda water. No ice.'

He smiled. 'You were always so confident.'

She ground her teeth. 'Until I met you and thought the sun shone out of your tailbone.'

Of course he ignored that too. 'You always had fire when roused.' They both heard the echo of a similar word. Was that aroused?

He held out her drink and she took it carefully, so as not to touch his hand. Again his gaze met hers and she looked away, knew his gaze never left her face. She could tell even with her fierce concentration on her glass.

His voice drifted over her like a wraith, encircling her, pulling tighter. 'But still there is more. Yesterday you were incredibly efficient. Practiced. Calm. Capable. All things I knew you would be.'

She didn't want to hear this. She wanted out. 'Why don't you cut to the chase, Stefano? Why are you here on this ship?' And, more to the point, 'Why am I here in your suite?'

He stepped closer. 'The truth?'

She shrugged, trying hard to disguise the fact she was getting more spooked by the second. 'Novel idea, I know.'

He came to stand in front of her chair. 'I could not forget you.'

'Spare me.' *Please don't say that,* she pleaded mentally. 'It took you nine months to figure that out?' Unobtrusively she eased back in the seat to create a little more space. Now she could inhale his aftershave, just a wisp, and it was true. The sense of smell was the one true memory.

He looked down. Apparently sincere. 'I did search for you.'

'For a prince with all those resources at your beck and call, you're not very good at it, are you? The searching-for-me thing.' She'd remained in the same flat for five months. Waiting. Hoping he'd at least call back. Until she'd woke up to reality. 'Tell me. When did this fictitious search occur?'

Thankfully he stepped across to the window that looked out from the stern of the ship and she could breathe again.

The glorious picture window framed the blue of the ocean, the trail of the wash from their ship, and the haze of land off to the east. And of course, thanks very much, the outline of Stefano's magnificent frame.

'It was many months before I could begin. Only now, through chance,' he added more thoughtfully, 'or fate, have I found your whereabouts.'

He'd waited *months!* Not in a hurry to find her, then.

Four weeks after he'd left, she'd discovered she was pregnant. Another fourteen weeks and she'd been desperate for him to call so she could share her confusion, share her joy at the promise of finally feeling as if she belonged to someone, share her fears and hopes with the father of her child.

Instead she had been completely alone.

But not as alone as she'd been when her baby slipped away one silent night. The doctor said her baby had a cardiac malfunction, a missing part so the growth could not progress, and she had accepted that with grief, like the lacking in the relationship it had come from. The grief had been worse because in the beginning she had been ambivalent about its coming. Had thought more of the complications than of her own child until it had been too late for fierce regrets.

And the due date was next week.

The ever-present ache squeezed in her heart. It was time to go before her control let her down. 'Great. Thanks for that.' She stood, looked him up and down, as though he meant nothing to her. 'You look well. Don't seem to be pining. I think you'll survive.'

He stepped closer, into her comfort zone. 'Is Hobson your lover?'

Suddenly they were standing chest to chest, a pulsing fission of air between then, so intense she almost missed the question.

What? Where did this guy get off?

But stoking up her anger was a good idea. Much better than sadness. Anger made her feel less trapped. Less baited by his need for control at this moment. Less weak.

Flippantly, with an airy wave of her hand, she said, 'He's one of them.'

The flare in his eyes stunned her. 'Then his position has become vacant.'

'Don't be ridiculous.' Blinking, she sat down again in shock. Any other man and she'd think he was joking. 'You can't do that.'

Wrong thing to say. She knew it as soon as it was out of her mouth. He didn't even have to say it out loud. Of *course* he

could do it: the power of the Mykonides in the Mediterranean had never been in doubt.

Her turn to back-pedal. She'd suspected he had this side, had just never been shown it before. 'Of course Will's not my lover.'

Stefano wheeled away to look over the sea again. The sea was unpredictable today, now they'd left port, like her feelings for this man, and just as dangerous. But he was behaving badly. She was no better, she thought, as she saw his shoulders sink in relief. So he did care. Surely he didn't really think Will was her lover, but maybe the concept had grown since his visit to the ship's hospital this morning.

Without turning he said, 'Is there a man in your life at the moment?'

He had no right to ask such a thing. She opened her eyes wide. 'Is there a man in yours?'

'Little witch,' he muttered as he spun back but there was amusement in his eyes. 'Why are you baiting me?'

She glared back at him. 'Because apologies and good wishes haven't appeared on the menu and that was what I was promised.'

Yes, Kiri thought with triumph, she had a point. And again, he was behaving badly. Why did this happen with the man she wanted to liaise and let go of?

He paced across the cabin, which suddenly didn't seem so spacious, and came to a stop in front of her. 'I sincerely apologize for leaving you without explaining my reasons.'

She nodded. 'And the phone calls you didn't return?' From the look on his face he didn't even remember missed calls.

He gestured with his hand. 'I did not get them.'

'Perhaps not. Or the emails.' Her tone clearly saying she didn't care anymore, she hoped, and she put her glass down. 'I accept your apology. Thank you for my drink.' She hadn't touched it.

So that was that. The wall between them was too great for them to part amicably but her expectations hadn't been optimistic. At least he knew where he stood. It was time for both of them to move on.

She stood. 'Goodbye, Stefano.'

But as she passed him his hand reached out and captured her wrist. *No. No touching. Not that.* His skin was hard and tanned and his fingers strong. But carefully loose as if to judge her response, would release her easily if she indicated.

She froze and lifted her eyes to him.

His thumb stroked the pulse on the underside of her wrist. 'Dine with me. Here. Tonight.' Her belly clenched and her legs weakened. Damn the man.

'No.' She tugged in slow motion, as if already unsure if she wanted release or not.

'Tomorrow?' He stared, his eyes darker than the depths of hell that she was falling into. Between them the fire flickered and stirred and the wraith encircled them both.

Throat dry she forced the words out. 'I'm working.' Almost a whisper.

He stroked her wrist again. 'Then it must be tonight.' Huskily, with another brush of her tongue over her lips, she wanted to say, *What part of no don't you understand*? But her mouth stayed shut and her body said otherwise.

For Kiri it was too late. Too, too late. He'd touched her.

The vibration between them made her forget the pain and seek the wonder. Wanted him to draw her into him like a whirlpool she couldn't fight against.

His hand held her wrist, his skin was on hers, and the two receptors were communicating, entwining in their own matrix of reality. The warmth crept up her body, wrapped around her in tendrils of mist, and in slow motion he eased her forward. Subconsciously she swayed like a reed towards him.

His other hand came up and tenderly brushed the hair out of her eyes. 'You have grown even more beautiful.'

With reverence his fingers slid across her cheek and along her jaw, heating, burning the skin, as his mouth came down, and she could do nothing but turn her face into his palm and then upwards. To wait.

As he had with their first kiss he took her breath, inhaled her soul as she did his, and the sometimes cruel world... Disappeared.

Her hands crept up around his neck and his hands slid down, until he cupped her buttocks and pulled her in hard against him. With the taste of his lips on hers, she could feel all of him, rock-solid against her, familiar — too, too familiar yet missed — and then his mouth recaptured hers in the way only Stefano's could.

She moaned against his lips, her mind blank in the thick sensuality only he could create. She forgot all her intentions, all her reservations, all her sanity, and when he lifted her shirt, swept it over her head, sighed at her lace-covered breasts, she gazed up in a sensual mist of buried memories at the man she'd dreamt about last night.

He carried her across the room and she hooked her legs around his hips. Her mouth was on his, starving for the fuel of life she'd missed, as they backed through the doors to the bedroom in a haze of heat and hunger and primitive surrender.

The fog parted briefly as he lay her down, stripped off his own shirt. She could see the muscled perfection of his chest, the fine sprinkling of dark hairs and the nipples erect with his desire. Quickly he protected them both. And before her brain could function sensibly he was beside her, stroking, murmuring his delight, kissing her mouth as if he would never stop, and she was lost again despite the insistent whisper that warned she would taste bitter remorse later.

Her hand ran along a deep-puckered ridge of unfamiliar scarring on his thigh, a myriad of other ones down his leg, and her hand stilled. But he swept her up again before she could investigate further and the moment was lost in the maelstrom.

Chapter 9: Stefano

S tefano felt the swell in his chest, the furnace of desire for this slip of a woman who, until he touched her, could hold her own. Then she was his. Always his. He sensed it, tasted the victory he hadn't known he burned for until it was upon him.

Clothes had fallen away, skin melted into skin, and heat seared between them as they reacquainted, shifted, joined. Together they cried out, until the sound died in the little death and she lay beneath him, limp and spent in his arms.

Then he moved again, slowly, savoring every tiny moment, every gentle trail across pearl-colored skin, every cupping of mounds and exploration of hollows. And always he returned to her mouth, her honeyed mouth that he could never have enough of, until the beat grew faster, the hunger more desperate, the climax more shattering, and again they collapsed.

Replete for now, in awe, still confused by the speed and urgency that had carried them both, he lay back with his arm under her, hugged her close, smiling and sated. Dreaming.

For the moment.

Until the drop of a tear landed on his bicep.

'You are crying?' Stefano felt the dagger of shame and turned to see her face. Kiss her hand. 'I have hurt you. God, no. I am a beast.'

Chapter 10: Kiri

K iri lay in shock. She'd done it again. One touch and she'd lost all will. How could that be? She was no young and foolish teenager, swept off her feet by a handsome man.

She knew what he could do. Had wept buckets at his hands before. If she didn't get out now she would lose what shreds of self-respect she could gather from the clothes strewn around the floor.

'I have lint in my eye. It's okay.' She eased out from under his hand and inched to the edge of the bed.

He sat up, the sheet falling from his glorious chest, his hand out. 'Let me help you.'

No. 'It was sharp and panicked, and she tried again in a calmer voice. 'No. Thank you. One moment.'

A plan. She had no plan except to escape. Not to let him touch her again. Her feet touched the floor and she scooped up her underwear on her way down to the bathroom, padding past the doorway in bare feet to where her shirt lay on the floor like an abandoned child. Like her abandoned child. She scooped it up. Hopped on one leg as she slipped on her panties.

God. What had she done? How had it happened? At least he had used protection... but then they had done that last time. She would get a morning-after pill. Make sure.

All stupid thoughts when really she should be worried about escape and remaining undetected by a ship full of people who knew her. She opened and closed the bathroom door noisily, yet didn't go in. Instead she hurriedly pulled on her bra and her shirt and slipped out through the main door as soon as she was dressed.

Outside she pulled on her sandals and smoothed her clothes. To top everything off, if somebody saw her leave the suite of a passenger her job would go. And she was due at work in an hour.

On the crew level she passed Miko, her friend from her first early days on the ship, when she'd been more than a little lost. He was another of her brother's confidantes, and the restaurant manager on the *Sea Goddess*.

She ran her fingers through her hair. *Nooooo*, she must look a sight. Miko raised his eyebrows, smiled sardonically, and walked on without saying a word. Did she look like a woman who had just left a man's bed? How could she bear the mortification of being seen in this state? Kiri hurried to her cabin in the crew's quarters and as she went she groaned.

Chapter 11:
Stefano

Stefano groaned. Those eyes, those limpid pools. He'd forgotten how her emotions changed their color from brilliant blue to dark violet when she was aroused. Or angry.

Which was it? No matter now. She'd gone.

He knew it before he left the bed and found himself alone in the suite. And now, instead of finding resolution, they were in deeper trouble than before. What the hell had happened? He pushed the heel of his hand back into his forehead. *Idiot. Monster. Scoundrel.* He had not meant this to happen.

It had been like this the first time he saw her. She'd arrived breathless, like a beautiful, vibrantly exotic bird, grabbing his attention so that he'd barely been able to concentrate on surgical technique. Her fierce intelligence had shone joyfully out of the most beautiful eyes in the operating theatre, as blue as the Mediterranean Sea at sunrise, and he'd been lost.

His time with Kiri in Australia had blurred into a golden haze of laughter and loving and lust, and even his responsibility to Aspelicus had faded for a brief while as he was carried along in her spell.

When duty had called he'd fully intended going back to reassess it all properly. Discover where that brief relationship might lead. Discuss and decide. He had thought it would be a matter of days before his return, but first there had been the accident, then the months of rehabilitation when the chance of losing the use of his leg had hung in the balance. It had all kept him away. As if the gods had intended they should both suffer for too perfect a match.

By then she'd disappeared. And more crises had arrived. Slowly his mind had been torn from her as well... except for that tiny halo in his heart.

But it was bad that he had hurt her. Profoundly. He could see that now, and deeply he regretted it. The trouble was that it seemed if he had an opportunity to hold her again he had no choice but to take it. Hold her. Lose himself. Lose them both.

This had to stop. This was not healthy. Not wholesome.

Because the way he felt at this moment he would destroy them both before he could stop the way he wanted her.

Chapter 12: Kiri

The next morning, as the ship moored at Civitavecchia for Rome, the clinic lay quiet.

'You okay?' Will looked at Kiri with concern creasing his forehead.

She forced a smile. 'I must have eaten something that disagreed with me.'

Like a morning-after pill that sat on her stomach like a rock. She couldn't rid her mind of the distant warning that this had been the only chance she'd had to carry Stefano's child again. She hated that thought in so many ways.

Will patted her shoulder. 'Take a sick day. I've got nothing planned and can cover your shift. We'll manage.'

'No. I'll be better with something in my stomach, perhaps. It's fine. I'll stay.'

'Why?' Will gently propelled her out into the empty waiting room and towards the door. 'Go. Lie down. Read a book. You're allowed five sick days a year and you haven't had one.'

She didn't want to go back to her cabin to beat herself up. To go over in her mind relentlessly how she'd allowed herself to be seduced, had reciprocated in the seduction, almost caused it by her weakness. That was an even tougher pill to swallow.

But she did feel miserable, and not just mentally. 'Okay, but I'll swap a day. I'll do one for you next week.' She looked at Will's concerned face and felt bad, but relieved. 'Thanks. I'll see you tomorrow.'

'Do you want me to send up some food?'

'You're a sweetie.' She offered a wan smile. 'No. I'm not sure if I'm up for food but I'll wander. See if anything looks appealing.'

At least she needn't worry about running into Stefano in the public dining rooms. Far too plebeian for a prince. Though, to give him his due, he just avoided public places to avoid drawing attention — he had no grudge against them.

Stefano had never played on his royal privileges or his power with her. Except yesterday, when he'd thought she was sleeping with Will. That had shocked her. There had been real possessiveness in that threat, and she didn't understand why.

If he'd wanted her — truly wanted her — then surely he would have moved heaven and earth to get back to her.

How hard was it to pick up a phone? To tap out an e-mail? Even a note in a stamped addressed envelope would have been nice.

That was the crux of everything. She hadn't meant enough for him to follow through and say he wasn't coming back. Though, looking at what had happened between them yesterday, maybe he'd just expected to drop in every couple of months or so and slide back into her bed.

She groaned and climbed the stairs to her room. As expected, when she got there it closed in around her.

Nope. She couldn't stay here.

Swiftly she shed her white uniform and stood in front of her small wardrobe. Brightly printed sundresses made her want to shade her eyes, and she winced her way along the rack until she came to a sleeveless loose black pantsuit. Perfect. It suited her mood. Suited her intentions if the absolute worst happened and she came across him.

Kiri looked at the array of food; cheeses, meats, exotic curries and colorful salads, seafood, her eyes rolled over them all and settled on the most innocuous item she could find. She grimaced and chose a banana. She knew they were good for hangovers and, while she hadn't had any alcohol, the Stefano hangover left her all kinds of miserable.

Her belly rolled and she glanced at her watch. Not time yet for her next antiemetic. That was the problem with morning-after pills. The nausea that accompanied them was pervasive.

As she wandered back out to the pool area, a redheaded pre-teenage boy scooted past, almost knocked her down, slowed, and called sorry over his shoulder. He spied his brother — obviously a twin because they looked so similar — closing in, and put on speed again. To have that much energy...

'Hey, slow down,' Kiri called after him.

Just then his brother slid past her, didn't make the corner, lost purchase as he rounded a post at speed, and before Kiri could tell him to slow down it was too late! The second boy's feet flew from under him and, unable to save himself, he slammed his head of red hair into the steel pole with sickening crunch.

Kiri stood, stunned, then her mind clicked into gear. She took two quick strides and fell to her knees to bend over him, but the boy had clearly been unconscious before he hit the ground.

Kiri hailed a passing waiter who'd missed the action and sent him off speedily to summon further medical aid. Apart from him there were very few people nearby. Until the last passenger she wanted to see appeared and strode over.

For the boy's sake she was glad. For herself, less so. She ignored the surge of nausea as Stefano approached and forestalled any comment other than on the present. 'Did you see him hit?'

Stefano nodded. 'If he has not fractured his skull he is very lucky. I will take the neck as we roll.'

Stefano placed his hands either side in case of spinal injury, and together they turned him carefully onto his side to keep his airway clear.

Just then his brother reappeared around Stefano's shoulder, his freckled face screwed up with fright. 'Is he okay?'

Kiri recognized him with relief. 'What's your name?'

'Mikey.'

'And your brother's name, Mikey? And the number of the cabin your family's in?'

The terrified boy stuttered out that his name was Chris, and the number, and Kiri repeated it to make sure she had it right.

'Okay. Go get your parents. I'm a doctor. Your brother hit his head and knocked himself out. We'll take him down to the ship's hospital as soon as the stretcher gets here and we'll meet you down there with your parents. Can you do that?'

The frightened boy nodded and sped off. 'Slowly!' Kiri cautioned him, and she saw him reduce his pace to a jog.

Stefano's mind rolled back the years to a moment he'd never forget. A time when he too had been terrified at his brother's lack of response. The feeling of being powerless to prevent an accident, to prevent disaster. His father's constant reminder that *he* had been the responsible one, something said in the heat of the moment and rescinded but it never left his mind, weighed heavily even now.

It was no wonder he needed to feel in control as a man. But he could feel that control slip away now, as this boy sank deeper into unconsciousness.

Kiri must have seen the sadness in his eyes, because she paled and he recognized the moment when she too felt the presence of impending disaster.

'You think he's critically injured?' she asked quietly.

'Theros was like that as a boy. Always rushing.'

She frowned, shook her head and concentrated on the boy. 'I heard the impact. Horrible. Wilhelm should be here with a stretcher ASAP, but he'll need to be shipped out.'

'I agree.' Stefano lifted the boy's eyelids one at a time to see his pupils and frowned. 'If we are that lucky.'

Will and Ginger arrived and Stefano helped them ease on a spinal collar and slide the boy onto the stretcher on a spine board. Within minutes they were all crammed in the lift on their way to the hospital.

Kiri could feel her own heart-rate increase as she watched tiny ominous changes in the boy. A flicker of a tremor in one finger. The shudder of an indrawn, suddenly laboured breath. Nobody spoke as the doors shut and they all watched their patient.

Will looked at her. 'He'll need to be shipped out immediately.'

Stefano checked the pupils again. 'There may not be time. Already one pupil is dilating.'

Will shuddered. 'So fast?'

'It happens.' He glanced up at him. 'Do you have the equipment for burr holes here?'

'Craniotomy? I guess so.' Will looked at Ginger, who nodded. 'But I've never done it. Cranial surgery's not a common thing on cruise liners. We should chopper him out from the wharf. Faster than an ambulance.'

Stefano shook his head. 'The preferred option is retrieval, but I do not like the look of this. It should be considered just in case.' They all knew even that took time.

'Kiri says you're a surgeon. We're in the Med. Are you registered here?'

Stefano nodded.

'If it's burr holes will you stay? Supervise?' Will asked.

Stefano nodded again. 'Of course.'

Kiri saw the limbs on one side of the boy begin to tremble, faintly at first, and then with greater intensity as he began to convulse. Stefano helped Will hold him desperately to keep his cervical spine stable until the seizure ended.

Chris's breathing slowed, stuttered, and the boy's condition deteriorated further even in the short time it took to descend to the hospital. Kiri's heart sank. To them all Chris's prognosis had begun to look horrifyingly bleak.

Kiri fought back the horrible feeling they would be too late and helped Ginger steer the trolley from the lift as soon as the fit ceased. That was when she realized the boy's parents had arrived before them.

Stefano hadn't seen them. 'The fits will get worse as the pressure builds.'

'What will get worse?'

A bluff redheaded man hurried across to them with his worried wife and Mikey in tow. Kiri gently guided them aside as the others pushed through to the hospital. 'Hello, I'm Dr Fender.' She took the man's hand. 'Is Chris your son?'

Worried grey eyes met hers. 'Yes. Mikey said he hit his head.'

Kiri nodded. 'It was a very nasty fall. I saw it. Dr Hobson and Dr Mykonides are going to examine him now. While they're doing that we need to know if Chris has any other illnesses or allergies that we should know of. Has he ever had any operations?'

The father looked at his wife and she shook her head, fear huge in her eyes as she realized the gravity of Chris's accident. 'I'm a nurse. Is he going to be all right?'

Kiri could only pray. 'I'm sorry, I can't answer that. He's very ill. He may have fractured his skull and torn a vessel inside his head. It looks as though he is building a collection of blood that is pressing on his brain.'

Chris's mother paled and swayed. 'Subdural hematoma?'

She did understand, Kiri thought. 'Our first preference is to fly him out by helicopter from the wharf because his condition is so critical.'

She looked at them, deeply sympathetic, but sensible to the fact they needed to know what was going on. 'As soon as the doctors have examined Chris we'll know if we have time to transfer him. He's already had one fit and his breathing is laboured. Dr Mykonides is a passenger, but also a very experienced surgeon. He will know what is best.'

Tears began to trickle down Chris's mother's face and her husband drew her into the waiting room Kiri gestured toward. 'I'll send the nurse out to see if she can get you something

while I find out what going on.'

'Thank you, Doctor.' The boy's father drew his wife and son under the shelter of his arms and Kiri felt the tears sting her eyes.

'I'll be as quick as I can.'

The father's voice followed her. 'Take all the time you need. We'll wait.'

She nodded, turned and prayed as she hurried in to join the others. Chris had to recover. She knew the pain of grief she'd felt when she'd lost her tiny baby and could imagine the worry *they* must be feeling.

Wilhelm had booked the retrieval team but they would be thirty minutes before arrival at the earliest.

'We'll lose him if we wait.' Stefano examined the depressed skull fracture on the rapid X-ray they'd taken while Kiri read out the boy's blood pressure and pulse. 'I believe less than fifteen before brain damage is irreversible,' Stefano murmured to Kiri.

Sadly she agreed. 'Systolic blood pressure's rising, widening of pulse pressure, and his pulse is slowing.'

The pressure inside the head was compressing Chris's brain down towards the base of his skull. At some point it would do irreversible damage.

Will nodded. 'Let's do it.'

Kiri looked at Wilhelm. 'I'll talk to the parents, get consent, while you and Stefano get scrubbed. The nurse can get him set up in the suture room. We can make this happen fast.'

Chris's parents stood up quickly when Kiri hurried into the waiting room.

'A helicopter's on its way but Chris has pressure from the blood building very quickly on his brain. Already his blood pressure is high and his pulse has slowed right down. Dr Hobson and the surgeon, Dr Mykonides, agree it is imperative to operate now to relieve that pressure. I'm sorry to have to tell you there is a real risk Chris might not survive his arrival at the hospital if we don't do something now.'

Chris's mother put her hand over her mouth and hugged her husband, and Kiri saw the lump shift in his father's throat as he gathered his wife in close. 'Then do it.'

Kiri passed them the consent form, and the father signed quickly. 'They're setting him up now. The object is to make small round holes in Chris's skull to let the pressure out and repair the bleeding artery before the brain is damaged. It's an emergency lifesaving procedure. We may be too late. Do you understand?'

'Just save him.'

His mother whispered, 'And afterwards?'

'A medical team will arrive to stabilize him and transfer him to a hospital neurological ward.' She squeezed the mother's shoulder. 'Do you have any other questions?'

The father looked at his wife and other son. 'Not now. He's in your hands. Hurry.'

Kiri nodded and did just that.

Back in the tiny operating theatre, Chris's head had been shaved on the side of the fracture and draped to create a sterile field. Will and Stefano were preparing the area with an antiseptic solution.

'Consent signed. They'll ask questions later. Please go ahead.'

The ventilator machine was breathing for him, but no anesthetic had been used because the boy was deeply unconscious. It would be Kiri's task to monitor that and Stefano handed Will a syringe of local anesthetic for the skin incision just in case.

Will hesitated and Stefano waved him on. 'Let's go. Inject the site. Make a three-centimeter incision through the skin. Separate the fascia.'

Will did so and the boy didn't move. His breathing sounded mechanically in the room and Kiri was glad they'd had time to intubate, because at least they could keep him going until the pressure on his breathing center was released.

She'd never seen the operation before, and Stefano kept a commentary going as Will performed the surgery.

'Control the bleeding with the diathermy. Use the retractors now.' They could all see Will's hands shaking but Stefano's voice was rock-solid. 'Exactly. Yes. Now drill the hole with the hand drill two centimeters above and behind the orbital process of the frontal bone.'

Will's hands shook more, and Stefano leaned across and steadied him. Ironically, Kiri could not have been more glad that he was here.

'This is good. You will be an old hand soon.' He glanced at Kiri. 'Observations?'

'Holding his own, just. Pulse forty. BP one fifty on forty.'

'We have a minute or two at the most. Faster drilling.'

Stefano's eyes narrowed and Kiri wondered if he was frustrated by Will's nerves. She couldn't tell and wondered if he might throw legality to the wind and take over.

Will continued with the procedure.

'Watch for the release of pressure.' Just as the words left Stefano's mouth a thin, powerful stream of blood shot upwards high off the table from the collection in Chris's head.

Will jumped back as it slowed to an oozing trickle and Stefano murmured, 'Good. Pressure is released.'

Will shuddered. 'No wonder his observations were going off.'

'Speed is essential. Now we find the bleeder.' Stefano pointed with tiny mosquito forceps. 'There it is. Tie it off.'

Will leaned in. Tying off vessels was something he was good at.

'Good. Now bandage for transfer.'

Chapter 13: Stefano

Half an hour later the emergency team loaded an almost stable Chris into the helicopter.

His

Stefano walked across to where the other boy watched the transfer of his brother. Red hair stood on end from his agonized raking and fat tears rolled down his freckled face. He knew the turmoil ahead and Stefano's heart ached for him.

Mikey looked up. 'It's my fault. I shouldn't have teased him. He wouldn't have been so angry.'

Stefano put his hand on the boy's shoulder, squeezed the bony ridge as Mikey dashed a hand across his eyes. 'It is hard to watch. Especially for you as a twin.'

Stefano struggled to fight back his own images. He couldn't bear the thought that this boy would go through the same remorse — the same desperate ongoing guilt — that he had.

'My brother was sick like yours once. And I tell you it is *not* your fault your brother hit his head. Boys run and chase, and things happen we have no control over. It could have been you that fell and he would not have been able to stop it happening.'

Mikey looked away from Chris to the man beside him and he did not look quite so woebegone. 'You think?'

He knew. 'You did everything right by getting your parents to the hospital. We might not have saved your brother without them being there so quickly to give their consent.'

Mikey sniffed and rubbed his nose with the back of his hand. 'I ran. I did what the doctor asked me to do.'

Stefano nodded and patted the boy's shoulder again before he lifted his hand. 'You did well. Your brother is strong and he has you.'

They watched the helicopter pilot start the rotors and soon it was in the air. Chris's parents came across to shake Wilhelm's hand and thank Kiri and Stefano and then, with Mikey, they climbed into a waiting taxi that would take them to the hospital.

Will turned to Stefano and met his gaze. 'Thank you.' He sighed ruefully. 'Though I wish you could have done it.'

Stefano smiled grimly. 'No. It is better to have the experience. One day another boy may need your skills and doing it yourself can never be replaced by watching. There were only seconds between the same result for you or I.'

Will nodded and glanced at the ship that shadowed them on the wharf. 'I need to report to the Captain.'

He glanced at Kiri, and then Stefano, but held his tongue. 'See you later.'

Chapter 14: Kiri

K iri felt as if she'd been run over by steamroller now the tension had been relieved by Chris's transfer. Suddenly it didn't matter that Stefano was the only one left beside her.

She'd watched him go out and talk to Mikey and hadn't been able to help overhearing some of his words. Now she saw him in a different light.

Today Stefano had been kind, thoughtful, and a steady teacher. As much as she hated to admit it, he'd seemed like the man she'd fallen for back in Australia. He'd been great with Will. And he obviously cared about the trauma to both boys.

Which left her with questions of where they went wrong. What had happened to them? To her and Stefano nine months ago? Didn't she deserve the same consideration that he now gave to an unknown family?

It didn't make sense that he'd stepped out of character and left her with no further contact after the week they'd had. Not without a good reason. Was there more she didn't know?

'Perhaps we should talk?'

'Somewhere public, perhaps?' Stefano smiled ruefully and she felt the mirror of her own response.

'Lord, yes.'

No way was she going anywhere near his bedroom.

Stefano steered Kiri to the rooftop coffee shop and chose a corner table behind an exuberant fake palm. Kiri didn't mind because she was feeling particularly pale and not very interesting as nausea elbowed its way back into her consciousness now she had time to think about herself.

Stefano frowned as he noticed her pallor. 'Do you wish for something to eat?'

Kiri's stomach rolled and she winced. 'No, thank you. Just black tea.'

'You are unwell?'

He leaned towards her and again she recognized the tang of his cologne. This time, unfortunately, it wasn't her stomach that reacted. Something much more visceral stood up and waved.

She leaned back into the greenery of the exuberant palm. 'Something I ate.'

'Strangely, my appetite for food is also absent.' His eyes darkened and she hated that, because she could feel herself weaken. And waken.

There was that damned glint in his eyes that she couldn't help but smile at. 'Stop it.'

He shrugged those shoulders and she looked away. 'So, I admit it is good to see you, Kiri.'

She wasn't falling into that one. 'No comment.'

His brows went up teasingly. 'So, comment on something else. You did suggest the need for us to talk.'

So she had, but now she needed to start with something safe. 'Do you think Chris will be okay?'

He shrugged, not with unconcern — she could see that — but with a glimmer of hope despite the contrariness of life. 'I will keep in contact by phone, but I think the surgery should have done the job before damage, and his vital signs maintained stability after the surgery. Tomorrow will give a good indication.'

She'd known that. But still it was good to hear the hope in his voice. A silence fell. She could feel his eyes on her.

'There is more you wish to discuss with me, yes?'

Well, he was right there. She should get it out and finished with. Dispel the questions that were beginning to eat at her all over again. She drew a deep breath and looked back at him. 'Why didn't you contact me after you left so hurriedly?'

The waitress arrived, took their order, smiled and batted her eyelashes at Stefano. He allowed her to walk away, and when she was out of earshot he leaned forward and said the last thing she'd expected. 'I was in an accident. Unconscious and then physically disabled for five months.'

He had her full attention as she searched his face. Now she could see them. Tiny lines that hadn't been there before, a few strands of silver through his black hair at the side of his face.

She had a sudden memory of that ridge of scar on his hip she'd fleetingly discovered yesterday. Her fingers fidgeted with the saltshaker, tensed, aching to reach across and touch his hand in sympathy. Luckily she was not that stupid.

She let go of the shaker and retreated her hand to the edge of the table. 'What kind of accident?'

'Motor vehicle. I spent several months in hospital. By the time I was discharged and could begin to sort what needed to be sorted you were gone.'

He laid his hand palm up on the table, as if to signal he knew she wanted to comfort him with touch. Like a coward she shifted her hand into her lap, and his fingers closed over themselves emptily as he sat back.

'By the time I could look,' he continued, 'I could not find you. I thought perhaps you wished it that way.'

He watched her face and she saw the moment he understood that she had, actually, by then.

Now the dilemma was hers. Would she tell him about her own little visit to hospital? No. She couldn't go there now. It was all too painfully close.

'I was on ship. Had my own family stuff happening. My brother suggested I try this. I made friends here, decided to stay a while.'

He sat back further, as if to illustrate the distance between them now. 'Life went on?'

She nodded, as if everything was decided that easily. All sweetness and light and smooth sailing. Not the way she was feeling. Not even close. 'As it does.'

'But now we meet again.'

His voice dropped like that warm and heavy cloak around her shoulders and mentally she shook herself at the spell he could weave just by words and cadence and his very presence.

Harden up, she reminded herself, and sat straighter in the chair. 'Life is still going to go on, Stefano. You'll get off the ship. I'll sail away.'

He leaned forward. 'It does not have to be that way.'

'Yes. Yes, it does.'

She wasn't stupid. She'd learnt her lesson. Yes, he'd been sick for a couple of months, but that had been months ago. No contact after that because she didn't count enough. Well, she deserved better than that.

'Why?'

'Because we're from two very different worlds.' It would always be that way, which was why she wasn't going to put her heart out there to be stamped on again. Or be seduced into his bed for the next few convenient days.

'Do you plan to be always a ship's doctor?' Now his voice had turned formal and his expression more difficult to read.

But she didn't need to read him. She needed to get out of here. 'No. I'm ready to move on.' Now. Literally. Today. She glanced at him. 'Funny how I feel so unsettled suddenly,' she said dryly.

His head tilted towards her. His eyes roaming her face. 'And where would you move on to?'

She shrugged. This whole scenario felt surreal. They were like two acquaintances, chatting over a cup of tea, ignoring the explosion of unbridled passion so recently in their past. 'Maybe I'll go for experience. There's always the other extreme to this — foreign aid medicine. Or I could move into family medicine with Nick back in Australia.'

He nodded. 'It is very beautiful there.'

'My family is there.' She shut her mouth with a snap as hurt from the past rose in her chest. Her eyes prickled. She did not want to talk about families with Stefano.

She looked away hurriedly, in case he saw something in her face, then went on brightly as she drained her tea. 'Or I could go back to Sydney to another hospital. The family home's still there.'

'I see you have put some thought into this.' He looked pensive.

She didn't like to tell him it was only since yesterday. His fault. All she had to do was resign.

The nausea rose unexpectedly and she stood. 'I'm sorry. I have to go. Now.'

He rose also, his forehead creased with concern. 'Let me see you to your cabin safely.'

Thankfully he couldn't. 'I'm in the crew section. Out of bounds for passengers. At least,' she swallowed and just got the words out as she pushed herself away from him, 'I will be safe.'

Her boss sent Ginger to check on her around four. 'Will wants to know if you're up for dinner in the officers' mess tonight. Captain's request.'

Kiri sighed. 'Bloody Stefano.' She didn't think she'd said it out loud but it seemed she had.

Ginger looked suitably surprised. 'Kiri! I haven't been here long, but I've never heard you swear.'

Stefano hadn't been here then. 'Sorry, Ginger, but stick around for the next three days and you might hear considerably worse.' *Oooohhh*, she'd kill him.

Ginger sighed dreamily. 'He must really like you.'

Yeah, right. 'He liked me before. For a week.' Indiscreet. She shouldn't have said that but she guessed most people could tell they knew each other a little. Even Wilhelm had noticed.

Ginger sucked her breath in as her eyes went wide. 'A prince!'

'Right. Stefano's bored and he thinks he can amuse himself before he disappears back to his little island.'

Ginger laughed. 'You can't really call Aspelicus a little island. It's got mountains and flatlands and casinos, even. And it has this massive village on the side of the volcano, a gorgeous palace, and a fab hospital.' She rolled her eyes in awe. 'It's the most amazing place.'

Kiri had to laugh. 'You've obviously been there?'

'Last year. I was knocking around with the in crowd with my on-again off-again boyfriend-gossip columnist, long story – and we ended up there for the Prince's Cup.'

'The horse race?' Typical. He had a race named after him.

Ginger nodded nostalgically. 'It's not just any old horse race, they race along a spit of sand at the edge of the island. And they raise squillions for the hospital with the evening black-tie balls and cocktails and champagne lunches. I swear I put on ten pounds over five days.' Ginger grinned.

'You obviously thought it worth the later dieting.'

'Absolutely. Anyway, Stefano looked pretty amazing as the host. I guess I have a soft spot and can't get over the fact you don't want to play with him.'

Kiri rolled her shoulders and rubbed the wooden block full of tension that was her neck. 'Because, after the fun and games, I'm left picking up the pieces.'

Ginger must have heard the truth because her expression changed to one of sympathy. 'He really hurt you.'

'Yes, but my fault for being weak.' How much did she wish she hadn't started this conversation? How wide was the ocean? How high was the sky?

'I'm sorry. Want me to tell Wilhelm you're not up to dinner?'

Kiri knew she'd have to go. 'It was a request from the Captain. I can't decline just because I want to avoid his very special guest.'

Ginger proved she still didn't get the power of royalty by asking, 'Why not?'

You just didn't do it. 'Because Stefano will blow it all out of proportion, I'll find myself in sick bay, and Will doesn't deserve the hassle.' She sighed. 'What time?'

'Seven.' Ginger twisted her hands. 'The nurses have been invited as well. Umm, do you think you could introduce me to that dishy Miko if you get a chance?'

Her friend Miko, who smiled as if he knew more than Kiri was saying. 'He's a heartbreaker.'

Ginger shrugged. 'I need someone to take my thoughts away from my ex. I'm not here for marriage. And I heard he was fun.'

'Oh yes.' Kiri grinned. 'He's fun, all right.' Thankfully not from personal experience but she'd seen the devastation in his wake.

Chapter 15: Stefano

Stefano kept thinking about the way Kiri had hurried away. Was she really nauseated — she had looked pale — or was she upset? Did she dislike him that much? All questions he would appreciate an answer to.

There was more going on than she had explained, he was certain of it, because deep in his gut he knew she was hurting — and he had caused it. It seemed it was his lot in life to hurt the people he loved. But how to ensure she would at least talk to him?

He might find out when he took the Captain up on his offer – the only reason he took him up on his offer – because he was reluctant to be the prince among the guests and had hoped to maintain a low profile.

Stefano watched Kiri enter with Hobson and the rest of the room faded. He thought she looked less pale than earlier, which was what he'd wanted to see, or that was what he told himself.

'Ah, the medical staff are here.' The Captain smiled. 'But of course you have shared high drama with them already. Dr Hobson tells me your advice and support proved invaluable. Have you heard any further updates on the patient?'

'Through my contacts I've been updated hourly on Chris's condition and he is improving steadily.'

'Good to hear.'

'Dr Hobson and Dr Fender were instrumental in saving that boy's life. And the nurses, of course. You have a brilliant medical team on your ship, Captain.'

The Captain visibly preened. 'I'm glad to hear it.'

'Of course Dr Fender and I are old friends.' His companion straightened with interest and Stefano chose his words carefully. 'We met during a consultancy I held in Sydney last year. I fear she is concerned someone might think she's consorting unprofessionally with a passenger if she's seen too much with me.'

The Captain huffed in dismissal, eager to dispel such a thought. 'Not at all. Fraternization does not apply with previous acquaintances.'

'I thought not,' Stefano said smoothly, 'but of course I'm glad to hear you say so.'

'No problem.' The Captain stepped forward to meet Wilhelm and Kiri as a waiter circled with a tray of champagne.

Stefano forced his grip on his glass to loosen. Still there was a distance between them that might never be breached, and still he was not sure how to repair the damage. All he knew was that he wanted back his rapport with Kiri. That after months of feeling flat and rudderless suddenly he was alive again.

Chapter 16: Kiri

Kiri's ears were practically on fire. It was too obvious the Captain and Stefano were talking about her. She knew it.

'Soda for me,' Kiri said, and took the glass with a thank-you nod at the waiter as Stefano and the Captain approached. She should have asked for something with a kick. She plastered a smile on her face.

'Prince Stefano has been singing your praises, Kiri,' the Captain said. 'And yours, Hobson. All of the medical team, in fact.'

Kiri could play that game. Nice and impersonal. 'We were lucky to have such a surgeon to consult with, sir.'

'Prince Stefano tells me the boy is improving consistently. There is real hope he will make a full recovery. And no threat of the parents suing my ship.'

She didn't care if Stefano saw how much that news improved her evening. It was worth coming just for the information. 'That is wonderful news about Chris, sir. And, of course, your ship.'

The impulse to share her joy with Stefano meant she couldn't avoid looking at him any longer. Naturally, he was watching her when she did sneak a glance. She searched manfully for a topic to deflect the pink that was rising in her cheeks. 'Your brother and his wife are not here, Your Highness?'

She saw his brows lower at her mode of address. 'Theros and Marla are watching the show tonight.'

The Captain nodded eagerly. 'The show is excellent. Of course the crew's pageant will be on in two nights. You must not miss it, Prince Stefano. Kiri and Miko dance.' The Captain sighed nostalgically, glanced around and gestured the restaurant manager over. 'They tango brilliantly.'

Kiri distracted herself by watching Miko cross the room. All the women smiled as he joked and nodded, more of a celebrity than the actual Prince. Kiri couldn't help her smile. He was such a hoot.

'Sir.' Miko saluted and the Captain introduced Stefano. 'I think you have not met our royal guest, Prince Stefano of Aspelicus.'

Miko made a very creditable bow and Stefano nodded his head.

Oblivious, the Captain went on. 'I was just saying how much I enjoy watching the crew's pageant and especially your dances.'

Miko gallantly turned to Kiri. 'It is all because of my beautiful partner. She is a feather.' He lifted Kiri's fingers to kiss her hand with consummate grace. 'You look ravishing as always, Dr Fender.'

Kiri grinned and pulled her hand away. Something made her glance at Stefano, who had narrowed his eyes at the interloper. All trace of good humor had disappeared from his face and she remembered the way he'd reacted to her quip about Will.

Kiri decided discretion was the better part of valor. 'I have someone who wants to meet you, Miko. Excuse me, Captain, Prince Stefano.' And she drew the playful restaurateur away before more damage could be done.

'Ho-ho, if looks could kill,' Miko whispered teasingly in her ear.

Kiri relaxed against him. 'You are a menace.'

Miko's voice dropped even lower. 'And you have been sleeping with the Prince.'

Kiri's cheeks flamed. 'Stop it.'

He shrugged. 'You have known him before, perhaps? He is very jealous.'

Jealous, or a dog in the manger? But she wasn't immune to the thought. 'That's his problem.'

'And mine if he thinks you care for me.' But Miko laughed. He wasn't stupid. 'And also a problem for you, too, my friend's sister.' He shrugged as they moved out of sight. 'So why do you fight this great attraction?'

'Survival.' And she hadn't meant to say that! 'Because we are from different worlds and he has hurt me before.'

'And Nick knows of this?'

Kiri felt like stamping her feet. 'Why does everyone think my brother has to know about my life?'

Miko shrugged. 'Because he will kill us if anything happens to you. Therefore,' he shrugged, 'it is purely selfish on my part.'

She had to laugh. 'You are so shallow.'

Her friend nodded sagely. 'That is true. But it's also true that is what you love about me. Come. Introduce me to this woman who wishes to meet me and I will let you go back to your brooding Prince.'

Kiri poked him. 'I'm sticking with you and I'm going to spoil your chances of seduction.' Kiri stopped when she found the nurse. 'Ginger, I'd like you to meet my friend Miko. I'm sure you've seen him around.'

Miko bowed. 'It is a great pleasure to meet you, Ginger. I believe this is your first cruise with us?' Miko lowered his head over Ginger's fingers and while his vision was obstructed Ginger winked her thanks.

The Second Officer approached and as Miko straightened he glanced at Kiri and grinned, 'Kiri? You are leaving us? I fear the Captain has placed you at his table.'

'Has he? How nice.' Not. Next to Stefano. Of course. 'I'd better go then.' She lifted her chin and turned to cross the room again.

The men stood as she approached and Stefano frowned away the waiter who'd moved to hold her chair.

As she slid into her seat she murmured, 'Seated by a prince. I am lucky,' and sat demurely with her hands in her lap. Stefano settled in next to her.

'Behave or I will not sit next to you.'

'You arranged it.'

'True. Because I can.' He changed the subject. 'I realize we have not danced.'

What had brought that on? 'Apparently you have to go out in public to do that.' Dog in the manger? Miko had improved her mood and she would have to thank him another time.

Stefano sat back in his chair and regarded her. 'Not always, but *touché*. Of course, I am happy to meet your conditions.' He gestured with his hand. 'After this, perhaps?'

Not likely. 'I'm afraid not.'

Silkily he said in her ear. 'And why are you afraid?' Thankfully the entree arrived at the same time and she didn't have to answer.

Stefano appeared not altogether displeased. Damn. Had she given him the impression she was afraid of her own response in his arms? She thought of it more as a healthy respect for the severity of their fierce attraction.

Not fear of him, of herself. Thankfully, the man next to her asked a question and she felt him turn to the lady on his left. She answered, the man nodded, smiled and answered a question from his other side.

Kiri turned to study the room. It was a black-tie event. The frocks fabulous, every color, and cut - some barely covering breasts and thigh, and a sprinkling of black and silver to provide a foil. Though the men in their midnight suits framed their women wonderfully and waiters circulated in dashing uniforms.

She could hear the conversation between Stefano and his table companion. The Captain's wife had been born in Sicily and had apparently visited Aspelicus before. Kiri needed to stop listening and trying to see what was happening out of the corner of her eye.

She looked happy to be seated next to him. Ha. Good. It amused Kiri to see him cornered, and the good lady looked so pleased she doubted he would be allowed to eat in his suite again.

Sadly, the Captain's wife enjoyed her food, and when the main course arrived, Stefano turned back to her.

'The Captain tells me you are off duty tomorrow when we dock. I will be flying out to Aspelicus for the day on a matter of state that will not take long. Perhaps this could be a chance for you to see my homeland?'

Before she could decline he went on.

'We would have time to visit my facial reconstruction clinic before we leave. It has facets of treatment that may interest you.'

She shouldn't be tempted, but his genuine passion for his work had always been evident and it called to the vocation in herself. 'How far is Aspelicus that you can fly to do business and come back the same day?'

He clicked his fingers. 'A mere hour's flight.'

The Captain's wife leaned across. 'You should go, dear. It's fabulous. And the Prince will look after you.'

Kiri muttered under her breath. 'That's what I'm afraid of.'

The next morning, as the ship docked in Livomo, after a night of mental flogging because she'd weakened, Kiri had to school the shock from her face when Stefano arrived at the gangway to disembark.

Dressed in a designer suit as black as his hair, with his royal chain of office flashing gold and precious stones in the sunlight, he looked nothing like the man she could lose herself in. Her first taste of royal bling and she had to admit he wore it well. Too well.

The passengers leaning over the ship's verandas seemed impressed too, if the flashing of cameras was anything to go by.

His man opened the door of the official car and gathered her in. It was a discreet luxury sedan, so hopefully people wouldn't gawk and point at them as they drove along. She slid across the seat, suddenly glad she'd worn her best trousers and a camisole with a jacket, because even though she was off the ship it looked as if this was a day when she'd need everything she had to keep her head above the water line.

'I'm sorry to have kept you waiting.' Stefano slid in next to her, and despite the gap between them on the seat she could feel the shimmering energy field as he settled.

'You made quite an entrance.'

He narrowed his eyes at her as if perplexed. 'How so?'

And didn't she wish she hadn't started *that* conversation? 'You look very princely.'

'At the risk of being simplistic, it is my job.'

Well, she'd asked for that. But he looked so overpoweringly regal she was feeling threatened by her own insignificance. Not something she'd ever felt before, which begged the question of what would it be like when they arrived at the palace, where he held considerable power?

Just the thought of feeling inferior made her spine stiffen. 'You said you have matters of state to deal with... What will I do while you attend to those?'

His gaze softened as if he sensed how unsure she was about their arrival. 'I had thought Elise, my housekeeper, could show you over the palace if you would like. She will no doubt burn your ears with her historical fervor. Elise is very proud of the island's heritage.'

So she was to be diverted to the housekeeper. That should keep her out of the way. 'She sounds interesting.'

He didn't turn to face her. 'She is, but if you are not in the mood for a history lesson you could relax in the library and browse. We have an extensive collection of original books collected by my mother.'

'Both options sound appealing.' But the history more so. She could sit in libraries any day.

Now he turned to her. Searched her face. 'I should not be long. It is a matter of signing papers that should have been ready a week ago, and the settlement of a matter which has caused my father some concern for too long. Hence my decision to be done with it today.'

The car drove onto the tarmac of the airport and eased smoothly to a stop. Stefano glanced out of the window. 'I hope helicopters do not worry you?'

'Not that I've noticed in the past.' *Never been in one.* She was quite pleased with her nonchalant tone, but seriously, how many people chose helicopters as their basic transport?

She'd been psyching herself for a sleek little Lear jet but there was not much she could do about their mode of travel now.

'I'll be fine.' Though it looked more like a large bumble bee than an aircraft.

To top it off Stefano had climbed into the pilot's seat and the lump in her throat tightened. His man opened the rear door. 'I'll sit in the back, shall I?' she murmured to herself, and allowed him to bow her into the helicopter with its royal insignia, her reluctance disguised because she'd always prided herself on her sense of adventure.

This definitely rated as an adventure. She'd bet there were hundreds of girls who would have changed places with her, and she wondered again why Stefano had manoeuvred her into accompanying him on this excursion. As soon as the pre-flight check had been completed, Stefano turned to check she had strapped in before he started the engine.

As the roar grew louder the little cabin began to shake and she resurrected the deep breathing exercises she'd learnt long ago during her obstetric term. Calmness at take-off seemed a great idea.

In through the nose all the way down to the base of her lungs, hold for three, and ease out through the mouth before breathing in again. She didn't care that the breaths seemed loud in her ears and that Stefano's man must be looking at her strangely.

Thankfully after six inhalations the flutter in her chest began to ease, and when she opened her eyes they were three feet above the ground and going up fast.

Everything happened very quickly after that as they rose and turned and soared away from the helipad towards the Mediterranean Sea. The shimmer of the waves below made her squint and reach for her sunglasses in her bag, and away to her left the hull of their ship over-shadowed the docks.

Islands dotted the horizon in tiny volcanic outcrops, some with soaring peaks and others quite low to the water.

After nearly an hour, during which she'd begun to enjoy the bird's eye view over the waves, she realized they were approaching a larger island, shaped almost like a whale, with the hump of a volcano in the middle and three separate areas of inhabitation. A long beach on one side edged a magnificent horse racing track, and she guessed that was where all Ginger's action had happened.

They approached the soaring volcanic cliffs and flew towards a turreted castle perched in a position impossible to assail without permission.

As she looked down at a ribbon of winding road that circled the cliffs, she guessed that was the way to the gate. And when she saw the tiny toy cars that clung to the road strips she wondered if that was where Stefano had had his accident. To the left were rolling hills with what looked like miles of olive trees and scattered small villages, and on the other side of the island it seemed there was a small city she barely saw before the sight was cut off as they approached the castle.

Her stomach contents rose and fell as they landed on a brightly painted H on the castle forecourt with a tiny bump. They were here. She blew out a relieved breath.

Stefano lifted his headset and turned back to her with the flash of a white smile. A man who enjoyed his time at the controls. Why would that surprise her?

The door beside her opened and she fumbled to release her seat belt as fresh mountain air rushed into the little space. Her companion had already climbed out. Stefano waved away the person in front of him and waited with hand outstretched to help her from the cabin.

'Welcome to Aspelicus, Dr Fender,' he said formally, but the twinkle in his eye showed he was pleased to be able to share this moment with her.

She had no choice but to lay her hand in his, and of course when his hand closed around hers she couldn't help the smile she returned. She really needed to learn to avoid physical contact with this man.

'Thank you, Your Highness.' She gathered her own control and looked around. 'Your castle is very beautiful.' The words replayed in her head. Even the conversation sounded surreal.

'I think so.' He turned to a tall grey-haired woman who had crossed to his side. Her eyes were warm and kind and she obviously adored Stefano. 'Elise, this is Dr Fender. Please care for her this morning, until I can return.'

'Certainly, Your Highness.' She inclined her head, obviously happy to do whatever he wished.

Stefano nodded and strode off towards another stairway, surrounded by suited figures, before Kiri even realized he was leaving.

So much for goodbye, Kiri thought. A bit abrupt in the leave-taking department, to her mind, but maybe she was being childish to expect anything else.

Elise waved her hand gracefully towards the main sweeping castle steps. 'This way, Dr Fender.'

Feeling a little like an unwanted package, Kiri lifted her chin. 'Please, call me Kiri.' She smiled at the older woman. 'And may I call you Elise?'

'Certainly. Welcome to Aspelicus.'

They turned and began to climb the wide stone steps. Sections of the stone had been worn away by thousands upon thousands of footfalls over the centuries.

Kiri glanced around. Everywhere the castle lay meticulously maintained, from its flowerbeds to lichen-free stone. 'The castle appears old but very beautiful.'

'Some form of the castle has perched here for over a thousand years, and thankfully all generations have continued to treat it with respect and care so that it remains as strong today as it has ever been.'

Elise glanced around and Kiri had no doubt that any fault found would be swiftly acted upon.

'And has Prince Stefano's family always been the ruling family?' She couldn't believe she was talking about the man whose bed she'd left only yesterday. At that thought the heat rushed to her cheeks, and she stopped to examine a particularly ugly gargoyle and breathe back control.

Elise's voice drifted over her shoulder as she, too, paused. 'Indeed. Which is rare. They have been fortunate in that their sons have been most virile, and capable of siring many lines.'

With a pang of loss, Kiri knew she could believe that.

'Now, with Prince Theros happily married, there is even more surety of the line continuing. And I'm sure Prince Stefano will marry before the year is out.'

Kiri frowned at that little pearl of information. 'Do you mean he *has* to marry?'

Elise inclined her head. 'It is by royal decree that the heir to the throne must marry by the time he turns forty.'

Dear Stefano must be thirty-nine. Ten years older than her. She hadn't realized there was such a gap in their ages, but since when had they sat and discussed mundane matters like his needing to be married by the time he was forty and only having a year to do it?

Instead, they'd made love. Passionate, soul-searing, love. Often.

Relax. Stop. Settle. Her mind darted like the birds swooping outside the windows and she had to remind herself to be in the moment.

It wasn't every day she had a private tour of a palace. Kiri tried to concentrate as they walked through into a vaulted main entry with impressive tiling in glorious Italian marble that seemed to shimmer with light. Their footsteps echoed away to the gold-trimmed ceiling that soared to a huge dome adorned with age-darkened seascapes in turbulent oils.

During the next hour Elise opened doors to lush apartments filled with gilt furniture and more framed artwork. Some of the paintings were so huge they covered entire walls, while the floors glowed with the subtlety of magnificently woven rugs from the Orient.

The throne room proved the most regal, with red silk walls, two huge portraits of a man and a woman, and an extremely ostentatious fireplace that seemed to be made out of solid gold adorned with the royal crest. 'This is where the current Prince, Paulo III, was married. That is the late Princess Tatiana.'

'She's very beautiful.'

Elise sighed. 'She was a wonderful woman.'

Kiri looked at Stefano's mother and saw her regal son in the same hooded yet piercing grey eyes. Stefano belonged to all of this. 'Everything is magnificent.' And totally terrifying.

Elise nodded and led her back to the main hall. 'It is a mission I take on gladly to keep it this way, but these formal areas are not the most comfortable to sit in. These are state apartments, for formal gatherings and the hosting of foreign dignitaries.' She gestured to a side stairway. 'If you would like to follow me, we will go through to the family apartments, where it is easier to relax. Perhaps a cup of tea would refresh you?'

Tea would probably save her sanity. 'Thank you. That would be lovely.' An overused word, but Kiri couldn't help feeling overwhelmed and trying not to show it proved exhausting.

The idea that Stefano had been so comfortable in her little two-room flat seemed ludicrous and hard to imagine. No wonder he sat blasé amongst the lavish furnishings on board the ship's biggest suite. It was nothing compared to his home. And yet when they'd been alone together, she'd felt there was nowhere else he'd wanted to be than with her.

She'd been delusional.

'The upkeep must be substantial?'

Elise frowned. 'It is a duty and a privilege worth paying.'

Oops. Of course it was. That's what royal families and their subjects did.

They went through a set of large stained-glass doors and suddenly the light and warmth of a much less formal area lay before them.

Much less intimidating. 'Oh, this is gorgeous.' Kiri could see a conservatory to the side, overflowing with lush green plants, and to the left a sunken lounge with a handful of plush cushioned lounges and chairs. There were flowers everywhere, and even the artwork proved modernistic and lighter, but no less magnificent.

'The late Princess, Prince Stefano's mother, refurnished this.'

'She had lovely taste.' Captivating Kiri's attention with unexpected touches drawing the eye in subtle places.

Elise sighed with pleasure. 'Our tiny country is fortunate that its ruling family is wise in the ways of fashion and finance.'

Kiri glanced around. *They'd have to be.* 'Very wise.'

'Yes. The family fortune has built since not long after the Doges of Venice began amassing their own fortunes. Before the family became the Aspelican monarchy, one distant uncle was even friends with the famous Venetian Marco Polo, and the island became an outpost on the routes of trade and gathered the riches of silk and spices.'

Elise waved at a wall full of glorious pottery from all over the world.

'Marco Polo,' Kiri said as she nodded. Good grief.

'But since early Greek times always the family has held physicians. The Crown was bestowed on the first Prince of Aspelicus because he saved the eldest son of the Italian King during a fever that all had believed would carry him off.'

Elise really did love her history, Kiri thought with a smile, and nodded encouragingly for the woman to go on.

'In every generation one of the family becomes a physician, and I understand Prince Stefano will be showing you his hospital this afternoon.'

And yes. Right. That was why she was here. 'He did mention that.'

'Prince Stefano does great work.' There was an extra thread of emotion in her voice that had Kiri turning back to look at her.

'Elise... Do you speak from experience, personally? Has he helped you?'

The housekeeper nodded. 'My son. After many miscarriages I bore my Paulo, sadly at the time with lip and palate deformity. Prince Stefano reconstructed his face.' The woman's face seemed to glow. 'My son is so very handsome. It is a miracle.'

Many miscarriages. Kiri could only imagine the pain. 'That's wonderful, Elise.'

The woman nodded eagerly. 'And his work is not confined to those who know the family. He will repair any child and do what he can for the damage that affects peoples' lives. He is a great man.'

'That's wonderful to hear, Elise. Thank you for telling me.'

What else could she say? No wonder Stefano had wanted her exposed to Elise. The woman hero-worshipped him. Kiri would hold judgement until this afternoon, but it seemed Stefano had had many reasons apart from his accident for not contacting her when she'd needed him.

There was so much to learn about him and yet so little time. And he had shared barely anything with her of his life here. She wondered if her exposure to Elise was the most he could do to begin to share.

By the time they had sipped their tea and eaten tiny pomegranate cakes a maid had brought, the glass doors opened and Stefano strode in. Suddenly the huge apartment seemed infinitely smaller.

'Ah, here you are, and I see you've had tea.'

Elise jumped up, wreathed in smiles. 'And cake. Will you join us, Highness?'

He'd changed into less formal dark trousers and an open-necked shirt so she could hopefully assume his royal duties were over.

'No, thank you.' He glanced at his watch and then at Kiri. 'I hate to rush you, but flights are easier to and from the island the earlier in the day we travel. Air currents become stronger as we go into late afternoon. Are you happy if we leave for the hospital soon?'

Rough air currents on the way home? Excellent. Not. 'Of course.' She tried to sound upbeat. 'Are we flying?'

'No.' He smiled as if he knew it was an act. 'We will be driving across as I wish to give you a brief glimpse of the scenery on the island. But we must get back to the ship as promised.'

Their trip to the other side of the island started with a winding descent from the castle — an exercise in S bends with the cliffs falling away to the side and the sea below. Not dissimilar from being in a helicopter, really. Stefano drove a little convertible with total disregard for the precipice, and despite a few gasps, on the whole Kiri knew she was safe. Which in itself she thought strange.

'I hope this isn't where you had your accident?'

He laughed. 'Nothing so impressive. I hit a cow on the way to the hospital.'

'What happened to the cow?'

'Sadly, it perished of its injuries. Or so I was told later.'

When he woke up?

At the bottom of their descent they drove parallel to the beach, and Stefano pointed out the famous racetrack where the Prince's Cup would be held the following month. She remembered what Ginger had said. 'A nurse on the ship says you have quite a social event with your race.'

He smiled. 'It is popular with the sophisticated traveler and with philanthropists. We raise more than enough money to cover the hospital's costs for that year as well as for several health research projects. Last year we raised money for a gynecological wing which opens in a few days.'

'Not just a party, then?' She liked that.

He shook his head. Twice. 'It is a week of tedious social engagements which I would prefer not to have to attend, but the good it achieves makes me appreciate the generosity of those who come.'

'Poor sad Prince. You don't have any fun? None at all?' She was teasing him. And how long since she'd felt relaxed enough to do that?

He flashed a grin at her. 'Sometimes. The race is fun. If you would consider joining me for the event, I think I could have more fun.'

She'd bet he would. 'While you make a fortune?'

'That too.'

Not a sensible idea. 'Sorry. I'm a working girl.'

He flashed another grin at her. 'I thought you might say that.'

There was something in his voice that made her frown, but just then they rounded a bend and turned away from the sea. Now they drove through rolling vistas of olive groves with grey-green leaves that glittered like stars in the sunlight and stretched away to the base of the mountain and a third of the way up its sides.

'It's beautiful.'

'It is. We grow only three varieties of olive here and Aspelicus is famous for the gourmet oil it produces. One of my ancestors proclaimed that every family must plant three olive trees a year. We have many thousands of them now.'

'When do you pick the olives?'

'We harvest in November. The whole island participates. It is all done by hand.'

She raised her eyebrows, and he laughed.

'I admit. Not *my* hand.'

She tilted her head, couldn't help smiling. 'But it doesn't hurt to have the Royal Seal on the bottle?'

He grinned. 'Not at all.'

The largest village, though really it seemed almost like a city, was clustered above the last of the olives and clung to the southern side of the mountain with red-tiled houses and larger official buildings secured to the rock with Aspelican determination.

She could see the spires of several large churches, and the main belltower of a cathedral soared above the rooftops.

'I love the narrow stone streets. I'll bet the roads are cobbled and cool in the summer up there.'

He glanced where she pointed. 'If you come back, I will show you. It is serene and very special. Most families go back hundreds of years and have lived in the same houses all that time.'

'And your family for a thousand?' She was teasing him, but she was beginning to see that he had a heritage he was responsible for.

He tapped his forehead. 'Elise has been giving lessons again.'

As if he hadn't known she would. 'Wasn't that the idea?'

He shrugged innocently, and she had to smile when he said, 'I wouldn't dream of boring you.'

Liar. 'You knew you wouldn't.'

The rapport between them hung undeniably and Kiri could easily have pretended he'd never been away from her. There was danger in that. Real danger. Because it wasn't true. He *had* gone away and left her to face the worst time in her life alone. The sparkle seemed to drain from the day.

'Why am I here, Stefano?'

'When I saw you—' He shrugged and the movement tightened his hands on the wheel '—I had the thought to show you my work. Perhaps for you to consider a change in your medical direction... even to consider coming here and working with me for a time.'

She shouldn't have been surprised. He'd already said they should spend more time together. Seems he'd been plotting to entice her to his island with the carrot of working with him in surgery.

Ill-advisedly, the idea held attractions, because the tiny fragment of surgery she'd seen him perform in Sydney had been incredible. And she knew he was an excellent teacher. Further evidence only yesterday in his direction of Wilhelm through unfamiliar surgery for the ship's doctor.

To have the opportunity to watch and learn from such a surgeon would be the dream of many a young doctor looking to expand her skills.

But those other doctors wouldn't be as fatally attracted to Stefano as she'd been, once—no, twice—before and she didn't trust him. She knew, fatalistically, that if she moved here and spent time with Stefano he would ensure she became more than an associate. She would become the Prince's adoring mistress.

She must have been silent for an extended time, because the car slowed, and she could feel his gaze on her face. 'Do not concern yourself. This discussion is for another day. Enjoy the moment without strain. Let me show you first. You are not obliged, nor should you feel pressured, to consider anything you do not wish to do. It is my foolish pride that wants to show you my work.'

'Your work deserves admiration.'

He shrugged. 'Though, I cannot help that I do not like the idea of you going off to live your life without the chance of at least sharing my own dreams with you.'

Life. Dreams. Chance. All dangerous words for Kiri. Empty words. What was he trying to do?

'Why me?' And how was she going to quiet her unsettled thoughts now that he had spoken?

His attention returned to the road. 'Why anyone? Why fate? Why now?' He was giving nothing else away.

They snaked their way up a final hill, and against the backdrop of marching rows of olive trees, a modern building sprawled elegantly over several acres, two-storied, and painted olive-green to blend into the countryside.

The closer they drove the more attractive it became. Now Kiri could see vine-covered verandas running around both floors, and the windows winked with white wooden shutters latched back against the olive walls.

'It's so pretty.' Gorgeous, really. Stunning.

'My mother's design.' Pride, unmistakable in the gesture of his hand and in his voice, threaded through with loss.

'You miss her?'

'Very much.' He kept his eyes on the road. 'She was the voice of reason and the one who did not hesitate to laugh at me if I became too serious. Perhaps that is why I find you a breath of fresh air.' He looked away. 'But then she could forgive me if I made a mistake.'

He looked thoughtful for a moment, shrugged and went on. 'She could not change my father, for he was trained differently, but she influenced me greatly with her humanity and sense of fairness.'

This unexpected insight into Stefano as a very young man touched her deeply. 'When did she die?'

He hesitated, as if it was physically difficult to talk about himself. 'When I was a teenager. An unexpected aneurism. Before I began medical school.'

His world was so different to hers but they had something in common. He had lost his mother around the same age as she had. She knew that feeling. The devastation, the aching void in the family, the feeling of betrayal at being left an orphan. 'I lost both my parents in a car accident.'

He looked shocked. 'I am sorry. I did not ask enough about you in Sydney.'

She grimaced to herself. The past wasn't a part of their time together. 'No, you didn't. But I understand your loss.' And there had been little time between work and bed for conversation. 'I had my sisters and Nick to look after me.' To look after the nuisance youngest sister. Though to be fair, Nick had never treated her like that.

'But it is not the same, eh? Without a mother.'

'No.'

But this was not what she needed to think about as her baby's birthday came closer, and she pulled her mind away from the fact that she'd finally felt complete at the thought of being a mother. That too she had lost. As she would Stefano when the time came — a huge reason not to risk losing her heart to this man again. She was so sick of loss.

But Stefano's past?

It was the last thing Kiri had expected. A royal tragedy — the loss of a mother he adored. Kiri began to wonder about the man who ruled this little principality — Stefano's father. A man who didn't forgive easily. Who'd been brought up differently from someone with a sense of humor, perhaps? It made her wonder what sort of life it had been for the young Stefano and his brother after their mother had passed away so suddenly. Aneurisms were always sudden.

How had his father reacted to her death? How had these events molded the man she'd thought she'd known? Would she find out before her ship sailed away?

But they had arrived.

Stefano stopped the car and vaulted over his door to come round to hers. With ridiculous flamboyance he opened it and held out his hand. 'Come. Let me show you my work.'

Kiri looked at his fingers, outstretched, waiting, and handed him her handbag.

Especially vulnerable after the recent disclosures, now was not the time to let herself hold his hand. But scrambling from a low-slung sports car was a little more difficult than climbing down from the helicopter. She achieved it, although not with elegance, and eventually stood beside him.

It would have been easier to take his hand. She ignored the tilt to his mouth and allowed him to lead the way.

The foyer of the hospital beckoned with a bright and airy welcome, studded with serene watercolor seascapes and lush potted greenery. The receptionist appeared and bowed, and Kiri was reminded that this man was accorded deference. But not from her. He seemed to cope with that remarkably well, really.

They were greeted by an auburn-haired woman with bright green spectacles perched on a snub nose. She had a stethoscope poking from the pocket of her white coat. 'Your Highness. Welcome.'

'Ah, Dr Herore. I hope you are well?'

'Yes, thank you.'

He gestured to Kiri, who stood quietly by his side. 'This is Dr Fender.'

Kiri and the young doctor shook hands, and she could tell the woman was wildly curious about her, but in a nice way, and that made it easy to smile.

Stefano strode forward and they hurried to catch up. His whole demeanor had changed again and it was easy to see he loved his work. 'How are my patients today?'

'Jerome has been very silly and picked at his stitches. He will not listen to me, but perhaps now you are here...'

'We will start there.' He turned to Kiri. 'Jerome is five.' He slanted a glance at her. 'An orphan, caught in a bomb blast. I have been reconstructing his face and chest. He has been very brave but is quite the mischief.'

They walked the length of the corridor and turned into another wing. The wooden floors glowed with the deep red of cedar and Kiri wondered where they'd sourced these building materials on an island this size.

It was a warm alternative to the marble everywhere else.

In the children's ward lay teddy bears and scattered bright red cars while happy circus animals adorned the walls. With his back to them, a little boy hunched over a red fire engine. By the set of his shoulders he was not happy.

Stefano stopped and tilted his head at the solemn figure. 'Jerome, what is this I hear?'

The child turned, and even in the shadows his surly face lit up when he saw Stefano. But the ravages of war were still apparent in the crisscross of tiny sutures that mapped his mouth and neck as he jumped to his feet and limped towards them in his striped pajamas. 'Papa,' he lisped in broken English, and Dr Herore bent down and hushed him.

'You must not call His Highness this.'

'All is well, Dr Herore. Until he finds his new family, I may be his papa. And how are you, my son? What is this I hear of scratching sutures?'

The little boy hung his head and Stefano tilted his chin with one gentle finger.

'No more of this. My good work and that of Dr Herore needs to be carefully nurtured. Like the plant you take care of for me. How *is* my plant?'

The boy looked up with worship and reached for Stefano's hand. 'See the plant,' he said, and Stefano allowed himself to be dragged towards the window. 'It goes well, and when it is strong, I too will be strong.'

'This I believe — and see how pretty it is?' They both gazed at the robust olive seedling in a red pot. 'I wish this for you, too, so you must promise not to scratch your sutures.'

'I will not.'

'Good. Now, climb to your bed and I will wash my hands. This is my friend Kiri. She is a doctor too, and I would like to lift the bandages on your chest and show her how well you are healing. If that is all right with you?'

'Okay.' It seemed nothing could faze his good humor now that his hero was here.

Kiri could barely restrain her smile. There was so much pleasure to be had from their conversation, but even in short acquaintance she could tell Jerome was far too serious to be amused with.

Her chest had grown tight at Stefano's unexpected rapport with the small child. But then he had been good with Mikey, too. It made her wonder why he had left having a family so late when he would obviously be a splendid father.

The smile slipped from her face and she glanced away from Jerome. Would this be her in ten years' time? Good with children yet childless?

'Perhaps we will be able to leave the bandages down today and the dressing will not annoy you so much?' Stefano looked at Dr Herore with question.

She crossed her fingers and said softly while the boy's back was turned, 'It would help. He has been very patient, but the bandage is chafing him and he will not let us touch it.'

When Stefano had washed his hands and donned the gloves that Dr Herore had laid open, a nurse wheeled in a trolley with dressing equipment.

Stefano spoke to Kiri, but his words were for Jerome, even though he didn't look at the boy. 'It makes me sad when Jerome does not let my fellow doctors and nurses look at his wound, because when I telephone for his progress, they cannot tell me.'

Jerome shifted guiltily on the bed, but Stefano continued to gaze steadily at Kiri.

'He has been brave and strong since he came here. Now we have repaired his face and neck and used skin grafts for his chest he will be as other boys his age when we have finished.'

'Except I will have learnt your English.' The boy held his head still as he spoke.

'It is not *my* English. We speak it here so that all you children may grow up with two languages at least. Now is the perfect time to learn.'

Jerome shrugged. 'I do not mind.'

Luckily Kiri's giggle drew a smile from the boy and not a frown.

'She's nice, your friend.

'I think so.' Stefano was engrossed in lifting the edges of the thick dressing carefully. The little boy's fingers clenched on the sheet but he didn't move.

Kiri stepped closer and slid her fingers across the sheet next to his.

Jerome looked up with gritted teeth and tentatively reached out and held onto her fingers as if to draw strength. Kiri's eyes stung as she studied the brave little face and saw his sheer determination to be good. When she glanced up, she saw Stefano had stopped his easing of the bandages and was watching her.

'Did I not say he was brave? But we will count to five—' he wagged his fingers at Jerome '—in English, before we start again, so that he can be brave.'

Gradually the extent of the chest wound was exposed, and Kiri had to fight not to dig her own nails into the sheet. Everywhere across the boy's sunken chest tiny sutures trailed over the livid skin like rows of tiny ants, pulling together what must have been an almost mortal wound.

'Ah. It heals well. Your big heart is safe again.' The wound was clean and dry, and the graft site looked well fixed. 'Dr Herore will check the donor site later today, when you have had a break from people disturbing your wounds, but you are on the mend, my brave friend.'

When it was done, Jerome let go of Kiri's fingers as if he'd never needed them and turned his worshipping eyes to his hero. 'That is good.' Then he broke into Lebanese.

To her surprise Stefano answered him fluently and the conversation flowed over her head.

While Stefano spoke with Jerome, Kiri was drawn to a cot in the corner of the room, where a dark-haired little girl with a bandaged hand heavily disguised by white crepe sat quietly. The little girl turned big, mournful eyes to Kiri and did not return Kiri's tentative smile.

'And what is your name, little one?'

Dr Herore spoke from behind her shoulder. 'Her name is Sheba and she is from the nearest village. Her mother comes daily. Sheba's fingers were almost amputated in an accident, Prince Stefano has managed to reattach, and we have great hopes she will regain full use.'

'She seems heavily bandaged.'

'This one we cannot stop from pulling at her wound, so it needs to be well out of her way. We are still worried it may become infected.'

Just then a small-boned woman trotted into the room. Until she turned sideways to curtsey to Stefano, Kiri didn't realize she was heavily pregnant.

'Ah, here comes Mama now. *Bongiorno,* Rosa.' The woman was panting a little as she arrived, and Kiri wondered if she was in some pain. Her face seemed especially strained, even though she smiled at Dr Herore.

'Ciao, Dr Herore. How is my little Sheba today?'

They all looked at the little girl standing on tiptoe in her cot, reaching out for her mother, and such was the anguish on her little face Kiri could barely watch.

'She misses you badly.'

'Si.' Rosa brushed away her own tears, heaved the little girl into her arms to comfort her and was almost strangled by the tightness of her daughter's grip.

Dr Herore dropped a hand on Rosa's shoulder. 'A few more days, until the risk of infection is gone, and she will be able to go home.'

'I know. She is so lucky to come here. And soon my new baby will be born and Sheba will be home.'

Stefano crossed the room and joined the conversation. 'Take care, Rosa. You are rushing too much at the end of your pregnancy. You must be well for this little one too.'

'Yes, Your Highness.' Rosa looked totally overwhelmed by Stefano and Kiri glanced at him, confused by the many facets of this man she had thought special, but still an ordinary man.

The silence became a little awkward and Stefano settled it for every-one. 'Time passes.'

Though Kiri felt he was very aware he was disturbing the mother's time, not his own. He nodded kindly, brushed the shiny hair of little Sheba, and placed his hand on Kiri's arm.

'Come, before we leave, I will show you the viewing window into our theatres. I am very proud of the idea.'

As they left Kiri glanced back at the children, at the warmth they all showed towards Stefano. As the distance increased, she could just make out the mother and child locked in an embrace.

'How did Sheba hurt her hand?'

'A dog attacked her — thus the risk of infection has been very great. She has many intermittent antibiotics so she cannot go home yet, which is hard. Her mother will not miss a day and walks four miles to see her.'

'Can't you send a car to bring her?'

He smiled at her censure. Shook his head at the idea of doing so. 'I offered and she declined. I will get Dr Herore to ask again. But I must be careful of the old ways of the village.'

'The children love you.'

He shook his head. 'They are away from their families. It is easy to grow attached to an adult they think will keep them safe.'

She didn't think that was it at all.

They left the children's ward behind and turned another corner to climb a tiny spiral staircase with intricate ironwork. The steps were narrow and looked incredibly old and frail for a new building.

Stefano saw her hesitate. 'As you see, these stairs have been restored. They are safe.'

'Okay. I believe you.' She was beginning to understand that Stefano took his responsibilities very seriously. And he didn't know yet, that he should have felt responsible for *her*.

He ran his fingers up the iron handrail and there was something so gentle and reverent in the way he touched the cold steel she couldn't help the memory of other times when she had watched his hands.

When he spoke she almost stumbled, jerked from the past, and he put out his hand to steady her.

Luckily it was only for a moment, and his conversation remained on the steps. 'They are from a section of the castle that crumbled in a landslide and had become dangerous. I had them transplanted to this spot. They are beautiful, are they not?'

She ran her hand gently over the balustrade. 'I've always wanted a spiral staircase.'

He smiled down at her. 'Come work for me and I could call it the Kiri Stairwell.'

So now he would name a staircase after her? Tempting, but, 'You never give up. I'm sure the others who spend so much time here would not be happy with such favor.'

He shrugged. 'It is my hospital. I do as I wish.'

That was the man she knew was under there. 'How disagreeable.'

He stiffened, searched her expression, and then relaxed at the amusement on Kiri's face. 'Perhaps, sometimes, I am. Even need to be.' It was a fact — not an apology.

They reached the top of the stairs and turned onto a landing with windows on both sides of a narrow corridor. The outward-facing window opened over the roof and the lawns, and the inward-facing windows gave a superb view of a pristine operating theatre. Even from here Kiri could tell Stefano had every latest device for his patients, for comfort, and for the surgeon's expertise.

She couldn't help but imagine working there. Working with him. 'Wow. I'm impressed. It's fabulous.'

Stefano looked quietly pleased by her response. 'I knew you would appreciate the promise of facilities like these.' He turned and his face grew more serious. 'Even in the few days I saw you at your work in Sydney, barely trained in advanced surgery techniques, you had the potential to be a great surgeon. Yet I find you on a pleasure ship?'

'And you.' She was flippant. 'Ironic isn't it?'

Chapter 17:
Stefano

Stefano narrowed his gaze, trying to understand. 'Perhaps you could share why this irony occurred?' He suspected she would choose not to enlighten him and he stamped back his impatience.

Kiri waved her hand. 'Things happen. Life throws you something you don't expect. Your path changes.'

Share something he didn't know. 'And what changed *your* path, Kiri Fender. When? Whom?'

'Tell me about the type of operations you have here.' She turned her back. Stepped closer to the next window. Blatantly changing the subject. 'Is this the only OR you have?'

'*Bah!* You are like a clam.' *He slapped the wall.* She was the most frustrating woman. He would never have believed it before.

She didn't turn even then. 'And you are used to getting your own way. Too much. And not this time.'

He studied her slender back. None of his people would have dared to turn their backs on him. It did not seem at all difficult for Kiri to do so. But he would not have her different even though she frustrated the hell out of him. He reveled in the difference, the challenges she presented, if only she would open up to share something of herself. To not constantly frustrate him with her changes of subject, her dismissive shrugs.

'So, we continue the waltz of secrets.' *Bah* again. He moved on. Only because he knew he wouldn't open this little clam at this moment. Later, he would learn her secrets.

'Operating theatres: We have two others — though one is really only used in emergencies.' He saw the slight loosening of her shoulders. She hid more tension than he realized. He would watch for that sign again.

She turned to face him. 'What emergencies do you have?'

'Most often the sudden influx of more than one patient. Mostly in times of war. It is word of mouth.'

'You are told of disasters?'

'I have a representative in most medical facilities in trouble spots where children are at risk. They contact my team and when information is gathered, we discuss if the child or children will be strong enough to withstand the journey. To remove a child from all they know is no light matter.'

She could certainly see that. 'Of course. How are they stabilized? Who brings them?'

Good. She was deeply interested. He relaxed a little as he let her into his world. The memories of many retrievals colored his response.

'I have a team who fly in and out when we hear of a case that would benefit greatly from our intervention. There is also a political team that works with governments to organize extraditions, and a medical team that goes in on the ground to source the patient from whatever hospital they are in. They are the ones who stabilize for transport.'

'That sounds efficient.'

They were paid to be efficient. 'Most times. Before they retrieve, my political team endeavors to trace parents and relatives, if we can find them alive, so they know the child has survived and is being cared for. We try always to leave a point of contact.'

He watched her lean her nose against the glass, and not for the first time today he wanted to turn her cheek his way and kiss those stubborn lips of hers.

'Your organization sounds amazing, but still, a medical crisis for a child... Losing their families...' She shook her head. Drew a breath that shuddered. 'The children must be terrified.'

'I am aware of that.' Something must have crossed his face because she looked at him closely. He turned away and took a step closer to the viewing window so that all she could see was his profile. He wanted to do more but his position in the royal family precluded his ability to do all he wished. So often he'd been called away. Left important caring to others and he hated it. This he did not wish to talk about.

'As you see, the other theatres are along here — but perhaps we should go.' He checked his watch. They definitely had to go. He gestured toward the door. 'Come, Kiri. It is getting late.'

Chapter 18: Kiri

She'd said something to upset him. The mood had changed, and it seemed there was nothing she could do about that now, as he marched her along corridors towards the entrance. In the distance she could see the children's ward. She wanted to revisit again just for a short time.

But he had moved on more than physically. 'I have asked the helicopter to meet us here. We'll fly back to the palace for lunch — there is a group of people I must meet with — then leave for the ship straight after.'

As they took off and soared across the tops of the olive groves it seemed surreal that her pilot was a prince, and she was the reason they were flying across these paddocks. How did she feel about that? Honored? Chuffed? Excited? Certainly not oblivious.

Well, she wouldn't be human if she didn't feel a little bit special, but no use losing her head over it. This was only one day. She'd just have to be careful to protect herself, because her senses were going into overload with all this information and attention he was lavishing on her.

She'd enjoyed morning tea in the intimacy of the family apartments and she hoped, if she was lucky, that lunch would be similar, only with Stefano present.

How wrong could she be?

Lunch was served in the formal section of the palace, and she could barely see him at the head of the table, let alone worry about accidentally touching him.

It seemed her escort — what a joke — was in great demand, judging by the procession of dignitaries that kept interrupting any attempt on his part to address his food.

There'd been a brief flurry of attention when everyone in the room had looked at her as she had been introduced to his father — a shorter version of Stefano, with bushy white eyebrows and scarily piercing blue eyes — and her composure had taken a beating as the older man had stared right through her.

Stefano had moved her on and then handed her over to Elise again, so she'd felt transformed back into parcel mode, and the island's hero had disappeared even faster than before.

She'd begun to have an inkling as to how busy his life was when he was home. Was this how she'd been forgotten when he left her? An accident, an accumulation of duties, pulled away from her by outside forces? His world was this, duty, public service, torn between his family's royal needs and his love for his work. And she? A woman in Australia he'd known for a week – was it so strange he hadn't returned. His glittering world was so different to hers.

But that still hadn't prepared her for lunch.

To say the lunch was formal was an extreme understatement.

She'd half expected a servant to bring in a whole pig, complete with apple in mouth, but they didn't. Thankfully. Not that they didn't have the silver serving dishes heaped with a myriad of exotic foods, and a multitude of crystal glasses bore sparkling wines and exotic mixes. And this was *lunch*. Not intimate.

The woman beside her constantly complained about how far down the table she'd been seated while the tall, good-looking man on her other side quivered with mischief. There was something about him that reminded her of Miko, the charmer of the ship. There was no decision on who she'd rather talk to.

She held out her hand. 'Hello. My name is Kiri Fender. A pleasure to meet you.'

He took her hand in his with studied gallantry. *'Bongiorno, signorina.* Franco Tollini.' Of course he raised it to his lips instead of shaking it.

His mouth lingered on her fingers. Kiri kept her grin behind her lips, but unfortunately, for the first time since she'd sat down, managed to catch Stefano's eye.

How amusing — for her, at least. The Prince seemed less than happy. She turned back to her companion, who had no intention of letting this opportunity go by.

Franco reluctantly returned her hand. 'I am part of the Prince's team. We transfer the children home to their parents when they are well enough to return.'

'So, do you have a medical background, as well, Franco?'

'Si. Dr. Tollini.' He shrugged with self-deprecation. 'I am a specialist in rehabilitation, but since coming here I have been performing some surgery.'

'At the hospital, here? Do you enjoy your work?'

He smiled. 'It is my world.' Kiri could see that. He did love his work.

'The children are incredible. And it is my job to take them back to their families after they heal and help them settle.'

She couldn't help thinking of Jerome. 'What if their parents are not there?'

'Then they are adopted into families that will take very good care of them. Our mission is not to lose them entirely.' His dark eyes flashed with fervor. 'We ensure their schoolwork is well catered for, and more often than not they will have better learning when they return, with opportunities for further study provided if they wish.'

Why hadn't she heard more about this place? Everyone should know. 'It seems a fabulous cause.'

Earnestness shone from Franco's eyes. 'Prince Stefano is a great humanitarian as well as a great surgeon.'

Another fan. How many were there? She was surrounded by them. 'I have heard the Prince is also an excellent teacher.'

'Spare my blushes, Kiri.'

They both looked up as Stefano sat elegantly down on her other side, like an unhurried lion settling to watch his prey. Goodness knew what he'd done with the person who'd sat there a moment ago, Kiri thought, and had a sudden vision of the woman being thrown into a dungeon by Stefano merely because he'd wanted her seat.

'Hello there, Franco.'

'Your Highness.' Strangely, with Stefano now beside her, Franco seemed to shrink and become a little less boldly defined.

Kiri realized the Stefano she'd thought she'd known actually sat with leonine ease at the top in his own pride. There was that king of the jungle analogy again. She could almost see his aura of power which grew more apparent despite the gentleness of his tone.

Stefano went on conversationally. 'I've just been showing Dr Fender over the hospital.'

Franco looked at her, and then at the Prince. He swallowed. 'I was just telling,' he paused nervously, 'Dr Fender about our work. She has not had a chance to mention she knows you or that she's seen the hospital. Or, in fact, that she is a medical professional.'

'How remiss of her.'

Kiri had had enough of this. The big men talking around her. She turned to Stefano. 'And how unfortunate that you interrupted our conversation.'

His eyes flared but his voice remained even. 'My apologies. But the helicopter awaits and we must return — or should we be delayed until tomorrow?'

He let the question hang.

Kiri blinked, decided she needed to be on that ship pronto and pushed back her chair.

One of the waiters nearly broke his leg trying to get to her to help but he was still too slow for Stefano. Solicitous and grasping her hand. Eyes steely.

The sooner she left here and returned to the real world the sooner her head could try to sort out the hundreds of different messages she'd been getting today which left her spinning.

'Goodbye, Franco. Nice meeting you.' Deliberately she held out her other hand, quite sure Franco wouldn't kiss it this time, with Stefano watching.

She was right.

Franco also stood. 'Goodbye, Dr Fender.' He bowed deeply. Not touching. 'Your Highness.'

Chapter 19: Stefano

'You really were obnoxious.'

Stefano nodded and smiled at the dignitaries who bowed as they departed. He ignored the hiss from Kiri beside him and kept her hand firmly in his. To hell with what the gossips said.

It had been a most unusual day. He supposed he should try to curb his desire to run through any man who spoke to Kiri, let alone those who actually kissed her hand, but he wasn't sure it was worth the effort.

He was beginning to understand the pirate tendencies of his ancestors when they'd captured women and dragged them off. His mother would have been horrified. Then he smiled and remembered something she had once said to him about his father's courtship.

Perhaps his mama would not have been so horrified after all.

When they reached the helicopter he waved the pilot into the front with his man and climbed into the back with Kiri.

'Not flying the craft this time?' When he didn't answer she said, 'I think I'll sit in the front.' Vixen.

He laughed out loud, 'I think not.' And helped her fasten her seat belt.

When he looked again at her face she was shaking her head. The struggle on her face suddenly gave way and she smiled too. They grinned at each other, and his relief was a warning about how much this woman's good opinion mattered to him.

That and having his arms around her.

He'd been fantasizing about that all day. Not his usual *modus operandi*. In a dream world it would be better if he kept Kiri in his bed — that way she would not mess with his head, just his skin. Even at this brief thought his body stirred.

In the real world, she'd just as likely say he should stay in bed and she would run the hospital.

But his prestige would suffer if others heard the way she spoke to him. He really needed to do something about that, but he wasn't sure what. He had a feeling that a direct order would give her the excuse to walk away.

She straightened her face and pretended to frown at him. 'I don't know why I was smiling. I am not happy with you. At all.'

He inclined his head and threw caution to the wind rushing by outside the helicopter. 'And there are things I need to discuss about *your* behavior. Perhaps we could examine this over dinner. Privately. Say seven? My suite.'

'Six-thirty, if you don't mind. I work tomorrow. And the restaurant will be fine.'

Chapter 20: Kiri

Kiri wondered if she'd gone too far. She'd been very surprised when Stefano had decided against piloting their way back to the ship, and disappointed she wasn't going to have the cooling-off period she needed to recover from his grabbing her hand like that and marching her onto the helicopter.

It had certainly surprised a few people — not least her.

The problem was as soon as he'd touched her she'd been captive, and it had nothing to do with force. She glanced down at her fingers in her lap. She wouldn't have been surprised if her hand glowed like one of those luminous fish in the deepest depths of the ocean they were flying over right now. It felt irradiated with his touch, still warm from his warmth, and she was still subdued by the leashed power she had felt.

She wriggled her fingers until his hand came in over hers and stilled them. She glanced up and saw the devilish gleam in his eyes grow. He knew. Her face flamed and she pulled her hand away.

Stefano smiled. 'You may choose the restaurant this time.' He turned to look out of the window.

They landed back at the airport without too many of the bumpy updrafts Stefano had mentioned. There were a few minutes' delay while they waited for the pilot to give them the all-clear to alight, and then their transfer by car back to the wharf beside the ship took no time.

Kiri could feel herself tense as she waited for the vehicle to stop. Suddenly everything felt awkward, overwhelming — the gulf between them, the hundreds of different examples of how Stefano's life differed from hers, and the fact his upbringing made him someone she didn't know at all.

She was a fool to think anything could come of falling in love with this man. She should never have agreed to dine with him.

'Thank you, Your Highness, for an interesting day. Excuse me if I rush off. I must check in with my colleagues.'

He leaned towards her and spoke over the noise of the ship's loud-speakers. 'Liar.'

She forgot her recent revelation and glared back at him. 'Bully.'

His eyebrows rose. 'Two hours' time.'

Thankfully someone opened her door to help her out and she could escape.

For the next two hours Kiri felt as if a huge clock was ticking inside her head. Each tick was louder than the previous one as the hands crept closer to six-thirty.

With an hour to go she'd tried and discarded a hundred excuses, each lamer than the last, and in desperation had taken herself down to the sick bay to see what was going on there. Nothing. The place was locked and empty.

She declined to ride back up in the lift. It was the hour for pre-dinner drinks and well-dressed men and women would be crowding the lifts for the next few hours. So she trod the stairs, hoping the exercise might burn off some of the nervous energy she seemed over-endowed with.

Nothing for it but to get dressed and get it over with.

The problem was she still didn't know what she wanted. If she was honest with herself, there were many reasons why she would love to go to Aspelicus and work.

Not the least that it was time to leave the ship, stretch her brain, learn new skills. But was it time to risk her heart again?

And why this week, of all weeks, when her guard was down from a countdown she'd been dreading? When she was feeling so fragile? When the hardest thing was keeping this secret from Stefano.

Chapter 21: Stefano

Kiri arrived for dinner in black. The demure effect of her high collar was thankfully assuaged by the keyhole yoke neckline that allowed a glimpse of the swelling valley between her breasts.

Stefano rose smoothly, as did his libido, and one glance at the *maître d'* was enough to keep the man away from her chair.

'Stunning.' He leaned over her shoulder as she was seated. Along with the subtle scent of spring flowers he always associated with Kiri, the view proved more incredible from this angle. He'd turned voyeur. He should be ashamed.

He smiled as he returned to his seat and looked across at her with a lightness of spirit he'd lost on a plane nine months ago.

Never over-awed she murmured, 'You look very dashing, yourself.'

As he studied the menu he wondered how she did it — lifted him from being immersed in business, too involved in matters of state, too focused on his patients. She made him remember he was truly a man who deserved a life that was not always lived for others. It was this quality that so intrigued him, tantalized his consciousness, because *with* her he felt unlike he did at any time without her.

They had two days left — not enough to throw caution to the winds, but enough to convince her she needed to join his team. And then he could see if they had a future. Already it was at that stage.

When they had both ordered, and the champagne had been poured, he raised his glass. 'To an interesting day together.'

She bit back a laugh. '*Interesting* could describe it. Interesting word-choice.'

'*Salute.*' He leaned forward, paused while she savored a sip from her flute. 'So, what did you think of my hospital?'

He watched her shoulders relax a little. It was as he thought. He needed to press the advantage of their common interests for now.

'Your hospital is amazing. I love your work and the miracles you create.' She leaned forward, her eyes on his. Said softly, 'I see your love of children.'

And then her eyes filled with sadness and he drew in a breath, his own heart hurting for no reason except that she was sad. His hand reached out instinctively for hers but she drew back. 'Kiri?'

She blinked and offered him a smile. 'It must be very hard for them away from their families.'

'Your soft heart does you credit. We do what we can to ease their loneliness, but know they must be healed enough before they return.'

'Of course. Otherwise the surgery has been pointless.'

He leaned towards her. Wanting to touch her physically, impossible with her fingers tucked safely in her lap, but having to be satisfied with holding her gaze. 'And if I offered you a position there? On a surgical team, learning what I could teach you... Would you be interested?'

'Is that all you are offering? Because I don't trust you.' She didn't trust him not to find a way to have her in his bed. And who could blame her after the loss of control so recently between them? Though, to be fair, that was not all him.

'It is a job offer. Yes. I believe so.'

'Do you?' She shook her head. 'If it was a standalone package, just that position, it would be hard to refuse.'

And if it were not, would she then find it easy to walk away? They were destined to be together. Finding her here was dangerous for both of them.

She had more. 'I've worked hard, I believe in the good I can do. I deserve respect.'

He acknowledged her fierce intelligence, searching between her words, sifting for weakness, assessing his own strengths.

'I want you to be a part of the team on Aspelicus but I won't push you for a definite answer.' Yet, he thought. 'Think on it, Kiri. Sleep on it.'

He took a sip from his glass and set it down. 'And what did you think of the palace?'

Chapter 22: Kiri

The palace. Kiri thought of his father's cold eyes. The long formal rooms. Her own feeling of insignificance.

Most of all she thought of Stefano's vast importance.

'Your palace is very beautiful.' Now to the more difficult part. 'I enjoyed my tour and learning a little of its history, but it's not a comfortable place. I wouldn't want to live there.'

'So where *would* you live?' He didn't seem surprised. Which, she hated to admit, was interesting.

To hell with it. Honesty was needed between them, at least in this, and she would continue the way she'd started.

'In the village. A walk across the fields would be a delight after a hard day in the OR. I could practice my Italian, or French, or whatever language it is they speak up there.'

'Italian.' He sat back with a smile. 'You are then thinking about the position and the advantages of living on Aspelicus?'

'And its disadvantages.' She didn't delude herself that he would marry her, or even that she wanted to be a princess, watching her husband from the other end of a long, long table of dignified guests. He'd always find other things/people/responsibilities more important than her, as had her parents and siblings with their important jobs.

But that was farfetched. Ridiculous even. They wouldn't get to that. She'd be watching from afar.

His brows drew together as he listened. At least he was listening. 'Disadvantages? I see none.'

The entrees arrived. She thanked the waiter for his impeccable timing. The advantage of having this conversation here, in public, instead of in his suite.

As they ate she changed the subject. 'Elise said you operated on her son. Was the defect a difficult one?'

'Yes. Full thickness and requiring several operations.'

He explained in detail and drew on the table with his finger, outlining the sections that had required repair. Again he made it easy for her to understand why and how.

She would learn so much, grow her skills so fast, the voice inside her insisted. But at what risk?

'His mother is thrilled with his recovery,' she said.

He watched her, dark-eyed and dangerous, answering her questions about the recovery process, but she instinctively knew his thoughts were sifting through ways to convince her to stay. 'Elise has had a hard life. She would have loved more children. As her husband has passed away that will not be possible unless she remarries.'

'She admires you very much.'

He turned the crystal glass in his hand. Swirling the liquid so it caught the light. 'She has worked for our family always. For the last few years as my housekeeper, and she expects perfection for me.'

Now, *that* brought up an interesting topic and she wondered if she should broach it.

And why not. In two days he would be gone and she would never know. 'Is it true you must marry before you are forty?'

His brow creased and she thought she saw a flash of some emotion, but it was gone too quickly to name. 'I wonder why she felt you needed to know this?' His voice dry, sardonic almost.

'I'm sure there are dozens of perfect future princesses out there for you.'

'A few.'

Inscrutable, he studied her and she held his gaze. Not easy but she wasn't going to cower. 'So, what happens if you don't?'

His hand lifted. Swirled briefly in the air before he brought it down again. 'I forfeit my royal inheritance.'

She sat back. Now that was unexpected. He didn't seem too perturbed. 'Would you find it hard to live as a mere subject?'

'I make my own fortune. I spend it on the hospital. I would have more than enough to live on, and I would still be a prince.' His hand lifted again. 'But, I could not leave my country for personal satisfaction.'

Her stomach sank and her appetite drifted away but she kept her expression blandly interested. She hoped. 'So, you will marry to suit the King?'

'Yes.' He smiled, but there was no humor in his eyes. 'There are several women of whom my father approves.'

She knew one his dad wasn't so keen on. 'Congratulations.'

'Are not in order yet.' He glanced at her plate, seeing the signs that she had eaten all she wanted. 'Dessert?'

'No, thank you.' She folded her napkin and placed it on her side plate. What now?

'More wine?'

'I don't think so, thank you.' They were so polite she thought, and took another sip of the mineral water she'd changed to before the main course.

'Good.' He signaled the waiter. 'Then if you have eaten enough perhaps we could go somewhere more private to finish this discussion?'

Kiri glanced around. The atmosphere was elegant, non-intrusive and discreet. Above all, safe. 'I think not. I'm very happy with the company we are in.'

If he was disappointed he didn't show it. He just waved the waiter away again, as if it was of no matter, then was straight back to the hunt. 'So, what is it you'd want from me if you took this position?'

He had brass, asking that. Was she to watch him marry a princess and be his work lady friend? 'I could ask you the same question.'

'Ladies first.' He gestured with his hand.

'No.' She lifted her chin.

'So stubborn.' He glanced away and then back, and she couldn't read the expression on his face. 'So determined not to show me the respect I am used to.'

He was right, but she didn't think she could change.

'I don't try to offend you. I respect you, Stefano, more so after today, but I will not give in to your need for control all the time.' *Because I would lose respect for myself.* And in the end that was all she would have left. *Herself.*

'Well, let me see.' He ran his eyes lingeringly over what he could see of her and smiled. 'The idea of working with you, watching your surgical skills grow, feeding your desire to repair and restore function, to watch you blossom into the surgeon I know you could be — that is enticing.'

Kiri could admit the concept was very attractive to her too. 'And for me also.'

His voice wrapped around her. 'As well, I wish to show you the beauty of my homeland with its depths that you can only begin to imagine. Celebrations like the Prince's Cup, the galas held after the harvest season, the saints' days and the markets.'

He opened his hands and she couldn't help but be enthralled with his passion for his island. 'What else must I see?'

'In my palace are long tunnels from the castle to the sea, works of art nobody views, buildings so old and manuscripts so holy and so fragile even the Pope agrees we do not move them.'

She did appreciate his deep pride, and the responsibility he took with his position, and she was not immune to the honor of his trust in sharing those things with her. 'That would be wonderful.'

'And...' He left it hanging.

'Is there more?'

Of course there was more that he wanted. And that "more" scared her the most.

'Yes. Then there is the heart of it.'

His eyes darkened and his voice took on a quality that made the gooseflesh rise on her arms.

'Then there is the woman who makes me understand the baser instincts of a bygone age. Who makes me remember I am a man not to be trifled with. A woman I burn to protect and long to conquer. I want the lot — and I don't want you staying half an hour from my bed in the village.'

She shivered. It was there. Plain speaking, as she'd asked. There was no doubting his intent — nor the fact that every nerve in her body leaned towards him as he said it. She'd asked for honesty and got it. With a vengeance.

Oh hell.

He shrugged his shoulders, as if he'd been discussing the weather. 'But I understand your dilemma.'

Holy Dooley — what could she say to that? 'I don't think you do.'

'Then please,' he inclined his head, 'do tell me.'

Where to start? With her mind blown by the fantasy he had conjured she was starting from way behind. 'I do appreciate your honesty.' *Sort of.* 'And I will try to reply with my own.'

'See.' He smiled and looked at her as if she was a wonder of the world. 'This is why you hold me.'

She shook her head, not willing to be diverted from saying her piece while she had some structure in her head. 'Our arrangement must be strictly business. My own residence away from the castle — in the village, if possible — and set work hours.'

He shook his head. 'I do not find that possible. A single woman living in the village would be prey to gossip and perhaps even harassment.'

Kiri laughed. Loudly. Put her head down to control herself. So old-fashioned. She couldn't believe he said that.

He shook his head at her amusement. 'In my culture it is different.'

Still smiling she said, 'The harassment I'm worried about lives in the castle.'

He sat back, dark eyes full of wicked amusement. 'It is not me you are afraid of, Dr Fender. It is your own base instincts and the fact that we spontaneously combust when we are alone.'

Didn't she know that? 'Exactly. But I did not interrupt you. Perhaps you could show me the same courtesy?'

He straightened, only half joking when he said, 'You are speaking to a *prince.*'

But she wouldn't be shut down. Not now. Not by him when so much was at stake. 'And I have been told that is why you like me.'

It was Stefano's turn to laugh. 'So what am I to do? See you through the day, toss in my lonely bed at night, only to be exposed to your unreachable womanly wiles again the next day? I think not.'

She spread her hands, borrowing his favorite mannerism. *'Impasse.* Your choice.'

He sat back further and a slow smile crossed his face. 'I will sleep on it. Though I will not sleep.'

She gathered her purse. 'Well, I have to sleep because I have work in the morning. Which reminds me — if you meet my requirements, I would need to give two weeks' notice.'

He studied his hands on the tablecloth. 'Not necessary. I will see that the cruise line does not suffer; if you leave with me it will be when the cruise ends in two days.'

By the time Kiri made it back to her cabin her knees were shaking. What had she talked herself into? When she'd left this same cabin two hours earlier it had never been going to happen and now, after one meal with him, she was negotiating contracts.

Crazy, dangerous, foolish woman.

She needed serious advice.

She didn't know who to turn to. Now would be the perfect time to talk to Nick, but her brother had his own life and even if available, they were at sea so her mobile wouldn't work. She couldn't talk to Ginger because of the risk of her capturing the scoop of the week for her ex-boyfriend's gossip column. And Will, while a great boss, just wouldn't understand.

But when she went to work the next morning, as the ship docked in Monte Carlo, everyone already knew.

Because Prince Stefano Mykonides had put in her notice for her and a replacement doctor was arriving tomorrow, when the ship returned to Livomo.

So, not only would tomorrow be the day before the one she was dreading for emotional reasons, now she would be out of work and out of her home.

Notice given? How could he do that? Had he not listened at all?

Ginger's eyes were wide with a grudging respect for Kiri's new notoriety, which didn't help at all. She looked at Will and her stomach sank at the worried expression on his face. She couldn't believe Stefano had been so arrogantly sure of her decision — plus so high-handed that he didn't think there would be repercussions.

Her brain circled and bounced with the shock and she couldn't think. It was a classic example of his privileged lack of thought. How could he not realize this would send her back the other way?

'It's not true,' she said, conveniently forgetting that she had already decided to finish work on the ship regardless of Stefano's offer.

Will touched her shoulder. 'Well, the new guy's coming and your resignation papers have been drawn up without the need for any notice.'

She looked for inspiration or explanation but there was none on Will's face. 'How could he *do* that?'

Will rubbed his hands together awkwardly. 'Easily, apparently. It's by order of the cruise line's owner.'

Kiri stared at him and through him, trying to see an answer. 'Can I reverse it?' Remembered the talk of a cousin.

'Apparently not.' Will shook his head. 'I already asked, because I figured it was something like that.'

She could feel incredulous anger building. 'Well, thank you for that.' She could not believe this was happening. At least Will had had some faith in her. 'Of course I wouldn't resign without telling you. I can't believe he's done this. Is he insane?'

'No. I don't think so.' Will rubbed the underside of his jaw. 'Just used to power. Owed favors by the owner.'

She needed to get out of this small room before she exploded. This couldn't be happening. 'I'll be right back.'

'You want me to come looking for you if you aren't?'

Will was beginning to get the idea that this man played hard.

She was about to say yes, then thought about the repercussions that didn't just involve her. 'No. I can handle it. You stay out of the firing line. He has just bought more trouble than he knows.'

Kiri fumed all the way up in the elevator. Halfway she briefly wondered if perhaps she should have taken the stairs, to at least try and calm down and heighten the chances that she would act rationally when she arrived.

That thought was vetoed.

As each floor flashed by on the control panel of the lift, she couldn't remember ever being this incensed, but the annoyingly persistent voice in her mind was suggesting again that this headlong course of action might not be the wisest one.

Well, to hell with that. He deserved a blast. A quick in and out might not save her job on the ship, but it was going to make her feel a whole lot better.

When the suite door opened she let him have it. 'How dare you?'

Wrong man. Blast!

She scanned past the shoulders of the bristling man in front of her and spied her prey at the windows of the suite. She took a step but came up against the surprisingly solid bulk of Stefan's manservant.

'Let her in, Manos.' Stefano's voice was even. 'Then leave.'

Which only served to incense her more.

She threw daggers at him as she waited for the hulk to get out of the way. 'You might want to keep him around for protection.'

'I think not.'

The man hesitated as Kiri swept past, but Stefano waved him on and the door shut silently after him. Kiri kept walking until she was a hand's breadth away from him and glared into his face.

'I've upset you.' Stefano watched her with a wariness born, she suspected, of unfamiliarity with this kind of scenario. About time he learnt.

'Brilliant deduction, Sherlock.' He blinked. 'As I was saying — how *dare* you hand in my resignation without my permission?'

He stepped to the side and picked up a half-filled glass of juice. 'Don't you think you are overreacting?' His voice sounded mild, but the thread of sudden amusement in it was a torch to Kiri's anger.

'Not yet, I'm not.' There was probably steam coming out of her ears — not that he'd notice.

Unperturbed, he shrugged. 'I saw you were worried about giving the correct amount of notice.' He crossed the room and sat down on the lounge, crossed his legs and looked up enquiringly. 'My cousin owes me favors. I have merely taken the matter out of your hands.'

She spun and stormed across the room until she stood over him again. 'Well, I want it back in *my* hands. And I'm giving you a straight refusal on the offer of a position while I'm at it.'

He remained impassive. 'Don't be foolish. You are far from your home. What will you do for a job?'

She lifted her head. 'I have plenty of options.'

That wiped the smile from his face. 'I'm sure you have.'

'What's that supposed to mean?'

He put the glass down and she could tell his temper had slipped a little. A little? Hers was way past that as she loomed over him as he sat, legs crossed, no man spreading for a prince. Even that made her more furious.

He leaned forward to rise and she stepped back – might be prudent to have a little space between them.

'Whatever you wish.' He rose smoothly, all leonine grace and height and took a step towards her, his eyes drilling into her soul. His mouth straight and hard.

Alarm bells began to chime exit songs. She needed to get her piece said and go. 'Well, know this, Prince Stefano Mykonides. I'm leaving this ship tomorrow, and I'm *not* going to Aspelicus.'

Then she spun on her heel and got out of there before she tossed him into the sea.

Chapter 23: Stefano

The door closed and Stefano stared at it. He should have caught her before she left, explained his thinking, but, with a sudden realization he had missed before, he had been in the wrong. Out of line. And to take advantage of her emotion would have made him more culpable, not less.

She was totally correct. He had no right to assume control. *Yet.* Difficult to remember when all his life decisions had needed to be made and he'd gone with them. Most times he chose the correct path. With Kiri it had been one false step after another.

He would need to win back her good graces. Right the wrong. Because she *was* coming to Aspelicus.

Late that afternoon Stefano waited around the comer beside the lifts. He knew she would be out soon. He could imagine the headlines: *Prince Waits to Pounce on Innocent Doctor!*

The door opened and she walked across the foyer from the hospital to the elevator with a nurse, who pressed the button for the lift.

Kiri's hands were full. At least she hadn't tossed his flowers out or left them in the waiting room.

It was a two-fold ploy on his part. Part one, to apologize in public with flowers. Part two, knowing if he made the bunch large enough she would have to take the lift to get them to her room. His plan to throw himself at her mercy would not work if he had to follow her up the stairs.

Amazing how devious he could be when he had to.

He waited until the lift doors began to close and then strode across the distance between them.

'Hold the lift, please.'

He pressed the button for good measure, in case she was quick enough to realize it was him. He slipped in between them as the doors shut. 'I'm very sorry.'

'You can't buy me with flowers.' Kiri pushed the bouquet towards him but he was way ahead of her.

He took them and handed them straight to Ginger. 'Would you be so good as to hold these?'

Then he turned back to Kiri and lifted her hands in his, squeezed and kissed her fingers. 'Forgive me.'

Her hands and her eyes were cold. 'Done. I've forgotten already. Now leave me alone.'

The lift slowed. His plan had not met his expectations. Again. Why did that happen with this woman? 'It was a misjudgment on my part. I have withdrawn your resignation.'

He hadn't, but he could do it very quickly if need be. He'd hoped for some response, but again she just looked at him coolly and that surprised him.

'I'm sure you haven't.' Her brows raised. Daring him to lie to her face again. *How did she know that?* 'But don't bother. If the cruise company can do that without my knowledge, I don't want to work for them. And if you think you can control my life I certainly don't want to work for *you*. Not everything is under your control, Your Highness.'

The lift stopped.

He watched from the back of the cubicle as she stepped out, and as she walked away he heard her say, 'I'll see you at the show. Please keep the flowers, Ginger.'

Chapter 24: Kiri

Monaco was a great place to buy a catsuit — one with a plunging neckline - even in a thirty-minute dash by tender after work.

The salesgirl had assured her it was latex-free - Kiri didn't want to brush up against Marla and start that whole scenario again — and the blatant sexual statement that she could wear what she wanted, in front of whoever she wanted, would annoy Stefano. She hoped. It was her last chance to do so.

An hour ago it had seemed like a brilliant idea. The final night crew's pageant always proved popular with the passengers because it was more personal to cheer for their favorite crew member, waiter, or cabin person while watching them perform on stage.

Kiri had been dancing at the pageant with Miko for almost four months, so there was little practice needed for their tango session. And this was the last night to end all last nights.

Tonight the theme was the *Lion King,* but any type of animal was acceptable. The skin-tight leopard print suit dipped low at the front and, with a sheepdog's tenacity, rounded her breasts up and pointed them in the right direction without the benefit of padding. She hoped it wasn't cold in the auditorium.

Now she was dressed, the garment appeared so much more blatantly revealing under fluorescent light, and Kiri laughed with a trace of hysteria. The suit left nothing to the imagination, she thought, as she stared at herself. Maybe she couldn't carry it off?

But this was her last night aboard. Kiri gulped one last time at herself in the mirror, then stepped out into the corridor.

The first man who saw her whistled.

It was lucky she trusted Miko to look after her, because this suit was designed to say one thing. *Come hither.*

Her exotic shoes clacked down the hallway and she wondered why the heck she hadn't brought a coat. But it was too late now. Maybe it hadn't been such a good idea to flaunt herself, but it had seemed the most efficient way of annoying her nemesis for the last time.

Ginger had somehow discovered that Stefano would be in the Captain's box in the auditorium, so he would have a good view of what he couldn't have. That thought straightened her spine.

Unfortunately, once backstage, Kiri had a hard time fielding the ribald comments because Miko had been held up with a disaster in the restaurant. Finally, she dragged Wilhelm to stand beside her so he could glower at anyone who dared to raise an eyebrow.

'Not so sure brother Nick would like this outfit, Kiri,' Will said in his measured way as he looked anywhere but at her.

Kiri felt as if she should pat his arm to comfort him. 'I'm a big girl, Will.'

'I hadn't realized quite how big,' he said, with a rare attempt at humor.

'Will,' she spluttered. 'Don't you start.'

Thankfully Miko arrived, all suave black panther, and took one appreciative look at her, bowed and kissed her fingers.

'I see we will be dancing for effect, my sweet. I will step up to that challenge.'

This was followed by a ludicrously wicked wink that had Kiri smiling again. 'Well, you only just made it.'

'Such is the drama of my position.' He squeezed her hand, noticed the chill of it, and rubbed her fingers between his own. 'Enjoy your last night. Be Catwoman for me. Hopefully I will not wake up in a dungeon tomorrow.'

Kiri's nervousness receded. Miko always made her feel better. Like a favorite cousin. Funny how she'd never fancied him and yet he was a delight.

'Thank you, dear friend. I promise we will have fun.'

She'd never see these people again, would never do anything like this again. She might as well give it everything she had.

She lifted her head and plastered on a smile. Their turn. The red light came on.

How appropriate for her costume, she thought sardonically. as Miko straightened and she put her hand on his arm.

He patted her shaking fingers. 'Good girl. Let's do it.'

Chapter 25: Stefano

Stefano conversed pleasantly with the Captain's wife. It was what he'd been trained to do. He'd promised to attend but he wished the night over, so he could return to his real world and decide on his next strategy for seducing Dr Fender.

His brother and sister-in-law were in high spirits and had enjoyed their short holiday. All survived without any further dire dramas or embarrassments. The music changed to the unmistakable beat of the tango, and Stefano, like every other male in the auditorium, drew in his breath and held it when Kiri stalked onto the stage.

He heard Theros say, 'Is that the doctor?' but his eyes never moved.

Her ridiculous tail twitched, seductively sinuous and provocative, and the lights caught the skin-tight shimmer of her perfectly luscious body. Her breasts gleamed high and proud, shimmering with stardust. Stefano's mouth dried.

Mesmerized, he followed every sway and bend, each drift and spin. The woman in silver was heating his blood to boiling point, and never had he wanted her more.

Then he realized every man in the room had their eyes glued on his woman and wanted her too.

The flash of a camera from behind him made him grit his teeth, and he resisted the almost uncontrollable urge to reach back, grab the offending instrument and smash it into a million non-recording pieces.

Instead, he clenched his hands in his pockets and remembered to breathe, letting the air out slowly and with intent. He repeated the process, as if he would feel better soon. Unfortunately, he did not.

While he could even admire the grace and precision of the dance, admire the rapport and impeccable timing between male and female, he would have given the crown jewels for it to end. He wanted her covered from head to foot at this moment, as his anger built, preferably bound and in the back of his helicopter heading for home.

As soon as the dance finished, to the most enthusiastic applause of the night, the rest of the cast came on for the final joint farewell and men whistled at Kiri all over again.

Stefano gritted his teeth as the crew sang their way through the final number. There was thunderous applause and he wondered grimly how much of it was for his little Dr Fender.

Finally, he could excuse himself, and with Olympian control he strode to the stage door just as she stepped out in a group. Thankfully someone had given her a coat. She was laughing as he approached, her eyes bright with bravado — and that incensed him more — but he was no fool.

Miko was the first to notice his approach. 'Here comes retribution.'

He said it quietly in Kiri's ear but she heard and turned, plastered a smile on her face. 'Did you enjoy the show, Your Highness?'

'Most illuminating.' He smiled at the crowd, moved in next to Kiri, and laced his fingers through hers in a statement nobody could doubt. 'What a naughty suit.'

He stroked her palm with his thumb and he felt the shudder run through her body. His fingers stroked again.

Chapter 26: Kiri

Kiri's legs almost buckled.

This was not what she'd expected. Battle-ready, Kiri found herself confused by his soft tone, by the damned weakness she always had when he touched her, and the come-down from the adrenalin of the dance. And that thumb, insistently vibrating at the core of her, in tendrils of heat from her palm, was blurring her mind so she couldn't think at all.

Still, he hadn't looked at her.

'If you would all excuse us for just a few moments? I'd like to speak to Kiri. We'll catch up.'

She had to hand it to him. He'd asked nicely, but the projection that instant obedience was expected was miraculous... though Miko looked more than a little worried as she handed him back his coat.

How the heck did Stefano do that?

Maybe he didn't even care that she appeared almost naked in some lights. She sneaked a look at his face, saw his eyes and the penny dropped. Uh-oh. This might be a good time to run after her friends...

Black pupils filled with sparks and his hand tightened on hers. 'I won't take up much of your time.'

If she could disentangle her hand she'd be able to think.

More people tumbled from the stage entrance and another camera flashed. Stefano swore softly — the first time she'd ever heard him swear — and let go of her hand to remove his jacket.

Kiri's mind began to clear the second they disconnected. She only had these few moments until he put his coat around her shoulders. The reality of the danger switched on like a light in her befuddled brain.

They were on the lowest level open to passengers, one below the gangplank, and there was no way he could get her to his suite unless she got into a lift. Technically, she should be safe if she didn't.

'No lift!' At least she managed to get that out before he captured her hand again.

He nodded. Directed her to the stairs — innocuous enough. Almost as if he knew, his thumb circled her palm again, and her will weakened as a brief lull in the flow of passengers gave them a moment of privacy in the bend of the stairs.

He leaned her back against the wall, captured her chin and kissed her — not with force, he even started gently, though she could feel the tightly leashed control, the simmering emotion as he seduced her with implacable intent. He kissed her thoroughly until she could barely stand, would have followed him blindly over the edge of the ship into the water below.

Then he drew her up to the next level and into a packed but serendipitously waiting lift. It was as if even fate was against her. The whole time his fingers were linked through hers.

Her head began to insist she take note. She looked around and whispered, 'I said no lift.' She tugged on her hand but he didn't let go.

He whispered back. 'If that is the worst I do then you will be lucky.'

The idea was scarily attractive.

'Could you let go of my hand, please?' She said it a little too loudly but it had the desired effect. Everyone turned to look at them and Stefano dropped her fingers like a hot potato. 'Could someone press five, please?'

Her ears burned from the attention but to hell with it. She wasn't going to be monstered by a royal bully even if she had pulled his tail deliberately. There was very real danger here — and not all of it was coming from him.

The lift stopped on her floor and she alighted without obstruction from Stefano. As the doors shut she refused to look back and took off, with her own tail in her hand, as fast as she could towards the crew's quarters.

The ship docked in Livorno at five a.m. Kiri woke after a restless night with her pillow screwed in a ball under her neck, her sheets twisted and creased and her body aching as if she'd done ten rounds in a boxing match. But worse was the mental exhaustion from dueling with Stefano in her dreams all night.

She crawled into the shower with a whimper, infinitely glad she didn't share her cabin with anyone else. It was both an anticlimax and a blessing that she wouldn't see Stefano Mykonides and his entourage leave the ship. Because despite her resistance he had invaded her heart again, and now she'd have to re-banish him.

Today was going to be almost as big as tomorrow. She had to say goodbye to colleagues who had been her friends, and she needed to find somewhere to stay tonight with all her luggage.

Then she needed to start forgetting the last week and sorting out a plan of action for work.

When she walked into the medical center Will gesticulated wildly towards Ginger, out of character right there, and judging by the amount of waving going on there was a problem.

'You guys okay?'

Ginger had tears streaming down her pale cheeks, Wilhelm looked red-faced and angry, and both of them turned horrified eyes to her in varying degrees of distress when she arrived. Kiri felt her stomach sink.

'Tell her.' Wilhelm's words vibrated with emotion.

Ginger twisted hands that trembled as she turned to Kiri, but no words came out except a whisper that trailed off. 'I'm sorry.'

Cold crept down her neck. Kiri liked this less by the second. 'Sorry for what, Ginger?'

Wilhelm couldn't stand it any longer. 'She's sorry she told your story to her sleazy gossip columnist ex-boyfriend. You and the Prince will be splashed across every newspaper and magazine that can manage to change their lead article in Italy today.'

Kiri felt the cold seep into her bones. 'What story?'

'That you had an affair with Prince Stefano. That you flew to his island the day before yesterday.' Wilhelm dropped his voice and his eyes, unable to look at her while he broke the worst news. 'And that he didn't come to you when you lost his baby earlier this year.'

Kiri felt sick. And faint. And incredulously angry. 'How the hell did you know about my pregnancy?'

Ginger looked as if she was going to be sick. 'My ex-boyfriend did some digging and rang me back. Thanked me. Told me that. Someone sent him a photo of you both last night.'

Kiri's mouth opened and shut several times before words came out. 'And you shared my private life to a newspaper?' She looked at Wilhelm. 'And you knew?'

'No.' He shook his head vehemently. 'God no. Ginger came to me. Told me what she'd done this morning.'

Kiri could barely follow it. All she knew was that the whole sordidly tragic story, the pain and anguish she'd suffered alone, was now up for discussion by any busybody who fancied reading about her. Her family. Nick. Stefano. Incomprehensible.

She felt the nausea rise in her throat. The pain in her heart. The horror. 'How could you do that? *Why* would you do that? I can't even begin to imagine what motivated you.'

'I'm so sorry.' Ginger sobbed the words out. 'Last night I'd had too many drinks. Didn't think it through. Josh rang me, asking for help. He said he was suicidal and he needed one good story to keep his job. I panicked. I love him and I was scared he'd do it. So, I gave him the best story I could find.'

'Mine?'

Ginger swallowed and then nodded. 'Yours. But I didn't know about the baby. You have to believe me on that.'

Kiri sank back into a chair in the waiting room and shook her head, unable to comprehend the ramifications of just how public this was. That everyone would know a secret she'd kept hidden from everyone... most of all Stefano.

'Are you sure they'll publish it? The Mykonides family has a lot of power.' Didn't she know that? With the thought came the first hint of light. 'Of course they won't publish, not without the royal seal of approval, and I'm not interesting enough to write about if his name isn't there.'

Wilhelm spun the computer screen around to show her. 'It's online already.'

That was when she saw the explicit glory of her catsuit, in full color, and Stefano holding her hand. She looked like a call girl.

'That picture...' Her voice tailed off. She put her head in her hands. 'My family don't even know about the baby.' She looked at Wilhelm, but all his sympathy wasn't going to help her now. 'Nick doesn't know, or my sisters.'

'Then you'd better ring him.'

'I can't.' She shook her head. 'I can't think.' An image of Stefano flew into her mind and she groaned into her hands.

'Stefano... His family. He hates the press.'

Running the gauntlet of the ship as she said goodbye was nothing compared to the reception the Italian newspaper journalists had planned for her when she stepped onto the wharf.

The flash of cameras and the surge of the bodies that crowded round her stole the breath from her lungs and she felt herself sway with the onslaught.

A car screeched to a halt. 'Enough!'

One voice, a whiplash of command, and four bodyguards, hastily shielding a central figure. The crowd parted and fell silent in shock as Stefano strode forward, dropped his arm protectively around her shoulders and swept her back to his car. Her luggage was quickly packed into a second car by Stefano's manservant.

As she slid along the back seat, the flash as the first photographer recovered ignited others, and the din returned full force as Stefano slid in behind her.

The door shut and both vehicles pulled away. The guards followed behind as Kiri huddled in the corner of the seat, shaking, tears thick in her throat as she tried to regain her composure in a world that had suddenly gone mad.

She supposed she should be thankful he'd come, but she had no idea what to say to him. Where to start. What he thought. Her head still spun from the ramifications of such a private airing of her deepest pain. Many women had suffered such a loss but it hurt even more to expose it publicly. Not just the memory of the physical, the cramps and the loss of control, but emotionally it had been traumatic. And now the world was privy to that pain.

Stefano's pain too. That she hadn't shared. And still, he had come for her.

Chapter 27:
Stefano

S tefano could barely see straight, barely think at all as he struggled with a feeling of betrayal greater than anything he had ever experienced before.

This emotional landslide did not happen to him.

He was careful.

In control. Master of his own fate and no one else's — because his goal in life was never to be responsible for someone else's downfall again.

But control had been taken from him. This news had been waiting for him as soon as he woke. His office had gone into disaster mode.

His security staff had arranged a different departure point for himself, Theros, and Marla from the ship, to avoid the inevitable press, and he had seen them to the airport and discreet safety. But he'd had to return for Kiri, though he wondered bitterly, did she deserve it?

All this because he had terminated her employment.

It was a smallness he hadn't expected. Fool that he was. He had been told many times, and even in the last few days by his father, that he should stay within the circle of people who understood the rules. And he had defended her.

Now all the world knew she had been pregnant. *His* child. Even when he had been in hospital she would have been able to reach him. His child had died at the time when he too had almost died. Another painful situation out of his control.

His anger burbled, bubbled, and boiled. If it was true. Had it really been his child? Had there been any child at all?

He sifted through what he knew, what had been written, and tried to discern what was truth and what was fiction even as she who had caused this furor shivered beside him. He would find out. He would keep her close until this all died down and she could not spread more lies about him.

Even he knew this was the wrong time to confront her; anything she said at this moment he would not believe anyway. But they'd been so ready to confront issues previously...

He should confront her, should demand some truths, but what would be the point when she couldn't be trusted to tell the truth. It seems she had so little respect for sharing the truth.

The hardest part was the fact that he had always been the one to protect his family from his brother's many scrapes. His way for making up the past, perhaps. By being the prince his father wanted and Theros could not be.

Because of *him*.

But this disaster, this horrific shambles, this was all his doing, his and the woman beside him. They had brought shame to the royal house.

Now he needed to be strong. Not weak. He repeated it in his mind. *Show strength not weakness.* The plan of action he had decided on was not the answer; but perhaps it would buy him time and stop the damage to his family until the truth could be ascertained.

Chapter 28: Kiri

Kiri could feel the anger and tension vibrating from the man beside her, emanating in waves, like a radioactive leak from a damaged core. Well, she guessed she had pierced his protective shell with the last news he'd expected. And hurt both of them. Even if it wasn't her fault.

'It seems you must come to Aspelicus after all.' Stefano's voice, coldly formal, as if talking to a bare acquaintance he disliked intensely, made Kiri feel even more alone.

'You will be safe there until all this dies down. I will not be able to ensure further damage is not done if you are to be hounded. The rest we will discuss later, when I can be sure I will not do something I regret.'

That stiffened her spine. As if she didn't have regrets. As if *she* had orchestrated the most public airing of her grief. Grief he hadn't even been there to share.

'Oh, it's all about *you*? *You* regret? Typical.' He shot her a look of loathing and she returned it with interest.

'I am not informed of this...' He broke off, as if he could not speak the word.

'Baby,' she supplied. 'Your baby.'

'If it is true. Yet you tell a newspaper.'

So that was what he thought. Again, typical.

'You think I would share my pain so publicly?' She turned her head and stared at the swiftly passing streets. Blinked away tears of anger. And disappointment. 'You really don't know me at all, do you?'

She couldn't believe he thought that. But then again why wouldn't he? It was all about him.

Now she was on her way to Aspelicus and too emotionally drained to fight any longer. Not what she would have believed possible less than twelve hours ago. The way she felt at this moment he could drop her off on the moon and she wouldn't care.

In another world, if her baby had lived, she would be waiting with bated breath for her labor to start. For her baby to be born. Instead, she was the instigator of an injustice to him.

She just wanted to hide. And cry. But she wouldn't give him the satisfaction. Instead, she stared unseeingly out of the window as they turned into the airport and drove onto the tarmac.

Before they alighted, he touched her arm. So briefly for her attention and then pulled his hand away. 'Your pregnancy. The one you lost. Was it really my child?'

Kiri turned her head and stared at this man she'd thought she knew, felt the pieces of her heart crumble into dust, and looked at him with such disgust he flinched.

Finally, after a long pause, he had the grace to say, 'I apologize.'

But it was too late. Way too late. Of course, he would think that.

How could she have ever thought she loved him? 'Too, damn late. Your Highness. It will never be unsaid.'

His implacable face stared at her. 'If so, then when were you going to tell me you were pregnant?'

She could do cold. She should be able to, because she felt as if her heart had frozen over like those lakes in Switzerland she'd always wanted to see. A place far away, never more than at this moment.

'When you came back to me. But you didn't. I tried to phone. Email. Letter. But with no reply, I didn't get the chance. Did I?'

Her car door opened from the outside and the helicopter beyond it looked almost reassuringly familiar. Funny how things could change in so short a time, and she was glad when he handed her coldly into the rear of the aircraft and climbed into the pilot's seat himself. At least she wouldn't have to sit next to his smoldering disapproval for the next hour.

Their ascent and the flight were a blur as she succumbed to the paralysis this morning had left her with. It seemed only a short time later that they were landing on the forecourt of the palace, and she lifted listless eyes to the gathering that waited for them.

Stefano opened her door and shielded her from the waiting throng. 'For the moment, of necessity and to save face for my family, we are engaged. Perhaps some of the damage can be repaired. The engagement can be terminated when enough time has passed.'

His statement hit her like a blow to the chest. Fake engagement. Save their face? Save *his* face, more like.

This day just kept getting worse.

'I'm not pretending any such thing.'

She would not be the outsider again, like her whole damn childhood. She wanted to fit. To be loved, not tolerated. To be the center of someone's universe, not a distant moon floating in his orbit until he was ready to evict her from his gravitational pull.

'It is not pretense.' He pulled a box from his pocket and lifted her unresisting hand, slid on the heavy stone. The ring hung like a shackle from her finger, a monstrous square-cut diamond, mocking her newly engaged status. 'It is temporary.'

'That's all right, then.' A semi-hysterical laugh slipped out. 'I'm used to temporary.'

His hand tightened on hers. 'Can you not see you have done enough damage?'

She felt so tired. Bone weary. What about the damage to *her*?

This time when he took her hand no sparks flew. Their misery separated them completely and she should be grateful for that. What did she expect? That he would take her in his arms and weep with her, say he was sorry he hadn't been there for her? Unlikely. But it would have been nice.

He turned to introduce her to those who waited.

She didn't understand any of this. How could a fake engagement help this situation? It would have to end sometime. But she tried to smile as she mumbled 'Hello' and 'Pleased to meet you.' Then she was towed across the forecourt to a line of servants, where another flurry of introductions was performed until finally it was over.

The wall between them must be visible to all who watched, but no doubt the loyalty of his people would color it differently.

Once inside the palace, Stefano dropped her hand and strode ahead, so she followed him up the inner staircase to the family apartments, more unhappy with every step.

They even passed the stained-glass doors without opening them — so much for her favorite place — and climbed another staircase to a redwood landing.

He gestured her through and followed her in. 'These were my mother's rooms. It will be expected that you stay here. There is a turret if you wish for a quiet place to sit until I return. A place to gather your thoughts.'

'You're just going to leave me here? Alone?'

His face softened a fraction and she thought he was going to say something less harsh, but in the end he shook his head. 'This whole thing is a fiasco. I must see my father.'

And then he was gone.

More of a tragedy than a fiasco.

Kiri stood, shivering, in the vast apartment with several doors that were closed, like strangers shutting her out. She didn't know what to think or do. She hadn't felt this numb and directionless since that night when her baby had left her.

So utterly and entirely alone.

Chapter 29: Stefano

Stefano strode away, but in the back of his mind was the picture of Kiri's white face and how small she'd looked standing alone in his mother's rooms.

He had to harden his heart to that because his weakness with this woman had caused all this. He must put aside the guilt that whispered to him that in truth he had not tried hard enough to touch base with a woman who had given him everything he had asked for.

And this new pain — this gnawing emptiness he had never experienced before — could it be the loss of something he had not thought would affect him so powerfully? But over it all was the disgust that he had let his family down again. That he could not forgive.

He wasn't sure where to start to repair the damage.

When he returned to her she had fallen asleep on the sofa. He sat opposite, watching her, emotions in turmoil after his father's disappointment and disgust.

As if sensing his presence, she sat up abruptly, ran a hand through her hair and tried to straighten her clothes. He watched, expressionless, as she gathered herself into composure.

'Do you feel better?' Not what he intended to say but it would suffice.

She blinked and sat up straighter. 'That depends. Was it all a bad dream?'

He wished. 'It is still a bad dream.'

'Then I don't feel better.' She slumped back.

He almost smiled. 'So, I must apologize for assuming you told the papers.'

The misery on her face lightened briefly and he knew he should never had assumed that Kiri would do such a thing. 'You believe me?'

He had the grace to look away. 'I have the truth from your doctor friend, Hobson, who has been concerned for your safety.'

She blew out a breath. Waved her hand. 'Naturally you believe him when you didn't believe me.'

He watched her gaze travel the room. 'How long do I have to stay here?'

The ring sparkled in mockery from the side table. He wondered how long she'd worn it before taking it off. 'Is the apartment as well as the ring not to your liking?'

She shrugged. Listless. He had never seen her listless. 'I haven't seen the rooms. And you haven't answered my question. In fact you've said precious little, and I've had just about enough of being kept in the dark.'

He was the one kept in the dark but this was better. She was gathering herself. But he had to protect what he could from more damage. He said reasonably, he thought, 'You must stay until this dies down.'

She shook her head and stood up. 'That doesn't work for me.'

It was his turn to sigh. 'Again, we are at loggerheads. 'And if I were to ask what *will* work for you?'

'Thanks to you, I am unemployed. I need to find a job.' She glared at him. 'Find a place to live. Leave this fiasco behind and get on with my life.'

He lifted his hand. Gestured to the room. To the world outside the tall windows. 'All these things you can do on Aspelicus.'

She shook her head. 'I'm not staying in the palace.'

He shrugged. 'For the moment needs must. But in a few weeks perhaps you could move to the village through the week and stay in the castle during the weekends.'

As she lifted her head to dispute that he went on. 'You will be undisturbed in these apartments, of course, but for the next two weeks at the very least we must be seen together.'

'I don't understand. How can that help this... fiasco, I believe you called it? Why perpetuate a myth that will be found out in the end?'

He stood and walked to the window. 'Because my father wants it done this way. He is old-fashioned. He and my people wish desperately for my heir and they are greatly distressed to think I would leave the woman who carried my child alone. The loss of that dream and the blow to my esteem has created a furor. If they think I am engaged to you then not all is lost.'

'Your father hated me from first sight. I can't imagine that opinion has improved with today's events. The way he stared me up and down the first time we met promises little rapport.'

'You imagine things. My father is very focused on the good name of Aspelicus. He believes I should marry a woman of similar social standing, but this is my decision.'

'And mine. Lucky it's temporary. Because I am not marrying you.'

'But you will remain engaged to me for the time being, because you owe me that much.'

She closed her eyes, as if in pain, and somewhere inside himself he felt that pain. He hardened his heart against the almost overwhelming urge to pull her into his arms.

Until she said, 'I owe you nothing.'

Too bad. 'Is two weeks too much to ask? For the damage that has been done? To the name of my family and to me, as a man.'

Chapter 30: Kiri

Kiri could feel the trap closing. 'Can't we just be seen together at the hospital? I can work with that.'

'In due course.' He stood up. 'For now, there will be a formal reception this evening. You are guest of honor. At seven I will come for you. The timing is poor, with the Prince's Cup next month and all the functions that require my presence.' He looked at her with a cynical smile. 'And now *your* presence too.'

She was sick of it all but too exhausted to fight.

What did it matter? She looked down at her crumpled clothes. 'I'm sure I'll look fabulous for the event.'

'One of our local designers will take care of everything. She has several outfits she wishes to show you.' He stood, his gaze narrowed. 'Please try for a demure neckline.'

She narrowed her eyes. 'Shame it isn't fancy dress. She might have a habit and I could go as a nun.'

'You look good in black.' His tone was less than flattering.

With a wimple? Thankfully she hadn't said it out loud.

He turned and departed and Kiri stared at the closed door. What was she going to do? She had no idea how to survive what he asked of her.

Especially the way she felt at this moment.

And the wall around him was so thick she couldn't see the man she had once thought she loved. How had this happened? She sat here alone, held on an island where the ruling family could decide whether she could go or stay. But she couldn't cry mistreatment as she took in the sumptuous surroundings.

No allies if she wanted to ask for help. She would not involve her family unless there was no other way out. Before she could think of any possible solution there was a knock on the door and a maid brought in a tray bearing a porcelain teapot and setting.

Kiri decided the world might look less disastrous if she at least drank something.

By the time she'd finished her tea the designer had arrived and she discussed Kiri's fashion needs for the next two weeks while Kiri just nodded and let her have her way. Dress and handbags had been chosen, undergarments arrayed, hats, gloves, and shoes matched and promised.

Apparently, Stefano had forgotten to mention the beauty technician who arrived to manicure, pedicure, and mini-facial her before the hairstylist arrived.

It was perhaps fortunate that Kiri felt like a rag doll, able to be pulled this way and that, because her brain whirred like an unfamiliar machine as she realized that she was officially engaged to a prince — albeit short term — even if the world thought she had trapped him into it. And she would be expected to know what to do. For the moment, she let them have their way. Perhaps externally she would look the part, and it required no mental energy from her.

To her surprise, all the attendants seemed genuinely glad to be of service to her, and she wondered why Stefano's subjects didn't hate her for putting him through the gossip mill.

But it seemed that despite what he had said to Kiri personally, Stefano had cast her as the victim, not the offender. If only he didn't believe it himself, because that shift would make this whole scenario so much easier to bear.

She didn't know if she could get through this without his support. Her emotions were shredded already, becoming more fragile every day — until here she was, on the eve of the day she had dreaded for months.

Never would she have believed it would be overshadowed by something else.

Even some direction on what she should do or say would be helpful in her current brittle state. How dare he not see how lost she was and how in need of support from him, no matter how pressing the affairs of state?

The only other person who might possibly be able to help her was Elise, but the housekeeper had been conspicuous by her absence and, given her extreme loyalty to Stefano, that was not surprising.

Just disappointing, because Elise was the one woman in the palace who would know what was going on. And maybe even understand how Kiri couldn't possibly be responsible for airing something so privately tragic. Elise might just understand because she too had lost her dreams of children.

At one o'clock the attendants had gone. A maid knocked and delivered a small salad and a roll for lunch, with a pot of coffee. Desperately Kiri stopped her as she was about to disappear.

'The housekeeper — Elise. Is she here today?'

'Of course, Dr Fender. Mrs. Prost lives in the palace and is on duty whenever Prince Stefano is at home.'

She should have known. No surprises there. *That's how he'd like me,* Kiri thought cynically, *on duty whenever he wants.*

She nodded. 'Lovely. Then could you ask if she has a moment? I would like to see her, please.'

'Of course, Doctor.' The maid curtsied and slipped out through the door.

When Elise arrived, not many minutes later, Kiri

wasn't even sure what she was going to say to the housekeeper. One glance at her impassive face showed Elise had been withholding her own opinion.

Kiri needed this woman as her ally — she had to have at least one in the castle, and nothing but the truth was going to secure that.

'Please sit down, Elise.'

The woman perched uneasily on the edge of a chair. 'I hope everything is to your satisfaction, Dr Fender?'

The lines were drawn, then. 'I thought we were on a first-name basis?'

'That was before you became engaged to Prince Stefano. It would not be proper now.'

Kiri sighed. 'Fine. I need you to understand that I would never ask you to do anything that would harm Prince Stefano or the royal house of Mykonides.'

The woman's eyes flashed. 'And I would rather die.'

At least someone could be relied upon to do what she expected them to. 'I had already guessed that.' Kiri smiled. 'It is good to have that said.'

She folded her hands in her lap. 'But I also need you to understand that I had nothing to do with publishing or giving the information that was printed by that newspaper.'

'So His Highness has said.'

She wasn't getting anywhere. The woman still distrusted her, and how could she blame her? 'Elise. I met Prince Stefano and we were very drawn to each other. As a woman who has lost her own children, surely you can see that a mother would not share her grief with the world as has happened to me?'

Elise stilled, stared at her, and finally nodded.

Kiri felt the first glimpse of hope she'd felt all day and went on. 'I believe the Prince is a good man and is distressed by the news. Did you know I tried to contact him? I had no idea his royal duties were so arduous, or that his recent accident was the reason he didn't answer me.'

She saw the moment Elise understood and finally sighed with relief. 'There is still a chemistry that neither of us thinks sensible. Now this has happened and for the moment at least I must stay here. Behave as his betrothed. I don't want to let him down again, but I need help.'

Was that an imperceptible relaxing of her face? Was she imagining just a little more warmth in the woman's eyes?

'I see.' Elise looked away to the tall windows for a moment and then looked back. 'And I am sorry for your loss.'

'Thank you.'

The relief almost toppled her, but Kiri forced her back straight.

Elise narrowed her eyes thoughtfully. 'Yes. You will need help. I will help.' She added primly, 'Also, I can say there has been a retraction in the paper, stating the fact that His Highness was gravely injured at the time of your miscarriage, and that he found you only a few days ago. Things do not look so bad when the true facts come to light. Legal action has commenced.'

Kiri could almost spare a thought for Ginger and her boyfriend. Almost? Nope.

Elise stood up. 'I can see that it will help if you sail smoothly through the next two weeks.' She paused at the door. 'I will return with your itinerary and discuss what is required of you.'

For Kiri at least, things improved after that. Elise's support, once offered, was beyond generous.

By the time Stefano came to escort his new fiancée to dinner she knew the correct curtsies, the names of the five most important people she would meet, and the itinerary for the evening. Even the menu.

It felt good to have a little more control.

And Elise's final suggestion had come in words from her late princess, 'God rest her soul.'

Eyes intent she held Kiri's gaze. 'This is important. See only one person or the occasion will overwhelm you. Look, speak and smile at one person and you will be in control of the room.'

Kiri nodded. Sound advice and she'd certainly try. Because it seemed that no help would come from the man who had let her down when she most needed him. *Again.*

Kiri wore a classic black floor-length gown, with just enough cleavage to say, *so this is why the man is smitten.* Her dark hair had been artfully piled on top of her head, and with her faultless make-up it all helped her composure to appear complete. Too complete. Because she felt like a figurine in a wax museum — incredibly lifelike but numb to sensation.

But she would get through this with Elise's help, and with no thanks to Stefano.

Chapter 31: Stefano

Stefano didn't know what to expect when he reached the door to his mother's rooms. He hoped Kiri was still not slouched in the chair.

When he opened the door, for the first time in his life, Prince Stefano Mykonides felt intimidated: she looked at him with such indifference his blood chilled.

Though, just in that first moment when he'd entered her rooms to escort her, her eyes had widened at his black tails and the royal sash, with jeweled medals flashing. But only for a moment before she'd stoked up her anger. Had she concentrated on the person, searched behind the regalia, and remembered the man who had left her without support in such unfamiliar and challenging surroundings.

'I am ready, Your Highness.'

His Dr Fender looked like a film star. A frozen goddess. Not herself.

The besieged and crushed victim whom he'd rescued from the press had been replaced by a self-assured, stunningly beautiful, poised woman waiting calmly and coldly to take his arm.

He glanced around the apartment as if to see the other person he'd expected. This new woman did not look out of place. The room could have been designed for her.

The grandmother clock in the corner chimed, jolting him back into reality. Now was not the time to mull over questions that required thoughtful answers.

'Of course. As you say. Let us go.'

She put her hand on his arm calmly as he led the way and her fingers did not waver, but he could feel the ice between them where normally there would be heat.

All rose as they entered. Kiri smiled slightly and nodded - not effusively, but that was good. She curtsied to his father with such gracefulness that even the women of the court smiled and Stefano felt his chest swell just a little with pride. This morning he would never have dreamed that she would carry this off so magnificently.

This morning there had been no pride to be had.

'She has presence,' his father grunted for his ears alone. 'But it remains to be seen if you have ruined someone else's life by your reckless actions.'

Stefano felt familiar guilt chill the pleasure he had gained in the moment and he glanced at Kiri. Something in her expression made him wonder if she'd overheard. He could only hope not.

When he seated her beside him she answered his questions, but there was still the distance that had been there since he'd collected her. A gulf so wide he could see no way of bridging it. He assured himself that was good. For now.

She seemed to prefer to converse quietly with the Mayor, on her right at the table, and yet he, the more practiced statesman, was too much aware of her. She'd thrown him right off with her coolness and grace.

The evening continued to unnerve him. He had been prepared to protect her, gloss over the mistakes she wouldn't see, but she required no help. Kiri nodded and smiled and held her composure with flawless ease. Though she excluded him in her conversations as she concentrated on one person at a time. He found it disconcerting and irksome.

He leaned down, inhaling her scent and bringing his mouth enticingly too close to her ear. 'I am wondering if there is to be any attention from my fiancée tonight.'

Subtly she drew back. Said so very softly, 'You'll survive without my attention. As I did without yours today.' She met his eyes, cool and unflinching. 'Did it occur to you I could have done with a little guidance from you?'

No, and it should have. 'My apologies. My duties constrained me.' His glance travelled over her. 'Though I see no lack in your instruction.'

'At least the little advice I was given held good.'

Especially if she blocked him out apparently.

She was right. He should have made time to reassure her.

That had been inexcusable and reinforced that muttered judgement from his father. But there was more of this night to get through before he could think on any of this.

Chapter 32: Kiri

K iri saw the glance Stefano shot to his father who frowned across at them. This nightmare of a night was a glimpse into Stefano's life and what he dealt with every day. She remembered his comment that his mother had been the lighter-natured of the two. Not so his father. She could see that his father was judging her, or perhaps even them. His face formal and stiff and ever watchful of Stefano. Despite everything, she felt herself soften and sympathize with Stefano.

She glanced across to the old man and unexpectedly caught his eye. She glared at him, glad the engagement was a farce, because she didn't need a person like that permanently in her life. His brows rose haughtily. She turned away.

If tonight's disapproval had been there all Stefano's life, she had sympathy for him. She'd seen this scenario at lunch, his father offering nothing that approved of all the good things his son achieved; no wonder Stefano could become tense with pressure. He must constantly feel his father's judgement.

She could sense him beside her now. Feel the awareness that seemed to inhabit the space between them even when they were not conversing. But she couldn't afford to lay her hand on his arm. Or express the sympathy she wanted. She needed to stay focused until she could return to the safety of her room. But perhaps she understood him a little more.

Luckily the gentleman beside her could converse easily, with little prompting from her. The Mayor of Aspelicus was one of the five Elise had mentioned, so she knew his role in the business. He did seem delighted with her knowledge and her appreciation of his heavy civic duties, and mentally she thanked Elise for her tutelage.

Eventually the older gentleman excused himself to answer a question from another table companion and Kiri had to turn back to Stefano.

He raised his brows. 'And how is my old friend Bruno Valinari?'

Kiri smiled, because in a lesser man he would have sounded almost petulant. 'He is well. And proud of his son, as he should be. And how is your dinner and your evening, Your Highness?'

His mouth came down level with her cheek and she tried not to inhale the subtle tang of his aftershave, because it floated too many memories for a state function. Tried not to look at the strong cheekbones and carved mouth as he drew closer.

'If I am not mistaken I see you ignoring me.'

She could play that game. 'How unusual for you *not* to see something.'

His eyes gleamed. 'So, my sweet Kiri, the claws are out?'

She did not want to think about that ridiculous catsuit. Kiri sat straighter in her chair and even leaned a little to the right to increase the distance between them. She kept the smile on her face but there was none in her voice. 'I'm not dueling with you at this table.'

Actually, when it came down to it, she couldn't. She didn't have the headspace.

She glanced around for a friendly face and Marla waved her fingers discreetly from across the table. Kiri realized she did have another ally in the palace. When people began to circulate, perhaps she could excuse herself and cross over to Marla. The chance to seek out her supposed future sister-in-law would help enormously.

She changed the subject. 'I see Theros and Marla are here. They look happy.'

Stefano turned to look at his brother and his face became more guarded. 'Yes. It is good to seems he grows less restless. Marla and he seem happy. She is good for him.'

That seemed a strange thing to say. 'Is he normally restless?'

He glanced around to see if anyone had overheard. 'That is also not for this table.'

No-go zones made life even more difficult, but what did she expect when in truth she knew little about his family? 'In that case it's your turn to start a conversation or I'll go back to Bruno.'

He smiled and inclined his head, and the appreciation in his eyes made the heat rise in her own face. She jammed the rising weakness back into its box.

'You look beautiful. And confident. I applaud you.'

'Please. Go back to mocking me, because compliments play havoc with my composure.' The words were sarcastic but held far too much truth for her liking.

She glanced at his father, who watched them both from under fierce white brows, and then back at Stefano. 'It could just be confidence from designer clothes and my own stylist.'

'Perhaps. Perhaps not. We shall see. Tomorrow you must meet the people. Two more critical children have flown in for surgery and I must go to the hospital. As soon as they are stabilized I will be in surgery.'

She wanted to ask more but he went on.

'Unfortunately, the new wing — funded by last year's Prince's Cup — is to be opened. Now I cannot be there and my father's advisors have requested you attend with him.' He mocked her. 'Are you free?'

As if she had anything scheduled. And what if she said no? But just the idea of getting away from the palace made her feel better. She thought of the hospital and her spirits lifted. 'Of course. And could I visit the children as well?'

His eyes shuttered. 'I doubt there will be time. You will be busy with your duties. It is only to be a short visit.'

The flattening of her spirits at his refusal to even consider accommodating her did more to unnerve her than anything the glittering room could achieve. That he could so nonchalantly ignore the fact that to visit the children would give her pleasure seemed so out of character for the man she'd thought he was. It hurt anew.

Someone spoke to him from his left and she sank back into her chair. Sank back, not relaxed back, because foolishly she looked along the row of guests, most of whom glanced her way every few seconds, and knew this wasn't her natural habitat. She'd never get used to it — didn't want to get used to it — because she disliked the grandeur, the formality, the opulence of it all intensely.

At this moment she also disliked Stefano intensely, and this was where Stefano belonged. Not her.

When she glanced down to the end of the table, a man smiled at her and she realized it was Dr Franco Tollini whom she'd chatted with at the palace lunch. She raised her brows and smiled and let her gaze drift away. Complications were too hard. Her head was above water — just — and she wanted to keep it that way.

She lifted her spoon and tasted the dessert but she didn't want it. Too much food. All too rich for her palate.

How did Stefano keep so fit? He was all lean muscle and power... and perhaps she shouldn't let her thoughts drift there while she was being watched by a hundred eyes. Thankfully, Bruno turned to her and asked a question. She did not want to lose herself in remembering just how weak she was when Stefano held her. Or how she had arrived at this moment.

Finally the long dinner was over. Nobody circulated, and Kiri had never felt more trapped. They bade goodnight to the Crown Prince, who glanced over them both coldly, and then to Kiri's relief they bumped into Marla and Theros. Stefano seemed reluctant to chat, but Kiri made a point of asking Marla how she was.

Before she could answer her husband chimed in with, 'Catwoman. Meow.'

Theros grinned at her and Kiri blushed. Stefano stepped in and took his brother's arm, steering him away. Kiri wasn't sure what had happened but she had space to fan her face.

She looked at Marla, who smiled apologetically. 'I'm well.' She glanced at her husband and lowered her voice. 'He's an absolute darling but he has no social skills.'

It seemed a strange thing to say about a prince, and Kiri couldn't think of anything to say in response.

'What about you?' Marla continued warmly. 'I thought you were so brave, coming tonight.'

That made her laugh for the first time of the night. 'I didn't have much choice.' She liked Marla, a lot, and she did hope they could become friends.

Before she could enlarge on that Stefano returned with a subdued Theros, and Marla whispered, 'Let's catch up tomorrow,' before she caught her husband's hand and led him away.

Something wasn't right, and Kiri frowned after them, but all she could think was that perhaps the younger prince had had too much to drink.

Stefano steered her in the other direction. 'Come. It is late and we both have a big day tomorrow.'

His hand was on her arm again, and she didn't know how much more of this hot and cold treatment she could take. Her physical awareness of him beside her only made her more cross. Judging by the way his hand came over hers on his arm, he might have picked up on the vibe that she was about to shake him off.

Chapter 33: Stefano

Stefano meant to leave her at the door and stride away. Because if he didn't there was a risk he would sweep her into his arms and forget everything. But he wasn't that man.

A man who had temporarily ignored the responsibilities of his station. Given in to instant attraction. Lost himself.

One week in Australia. One night on a cruise ship.

Twice in his life he had allowed his heart to rule his head and look what had happened. But he could not rid himself of the look of hurt in Kiri's eyes, and his own heart ached in a way he had never experienced before.

When he let her go to open the doors to her suite, Kiri paused as he looked down at her. She stared at him, as if trying to see beneath his skin, and the moment stilled. The ever-present sounds of the grand-mother clock faded and their eyes met and held.

Here they were, and for the first time that evening, alone and unwatched. Stefano had time to feel like pulling her head into his to mourn what they had lost. How had they found themselves at such loggerheads? How had they ended up here, "temporarily engaged"?

Why had fate mocked them both and put such obstacles in the way of a woman and a man who were so intensely attracted?

'What happened to us, Stefano?' Kiri asked carefully.

Again he let her down. He knew it as he did it. Just compressed his lips and shuttered his eyes. 'Almost everything. We must try to make the best of this disastrous situation while I deal with it.'

Her temper flared. He saw. Had seen a lot of it these last days. He'd had no idea. 'I am not a "disastrous situation." I am a respected medical practitioner who has been kidnapped.'

He glanced around to check again they were still alone before he steered her through into the rooms, closed the doors and stood with his back to them. 'Please try and remember what happens when people overhear things they shouldn't.'

'I, of all people, am sick of worrying about what others think. Why do you think you can shut me out? Why do you need to control everything? Do you think it actually changes fate? Life is learning to live with what happens. And for goodness sake, one of us needs to be honest.'

'This is a disaster. Listen now. This minute I am honest with you.'

She gestured to the room. '*You're* different. Everything is different here. Especially now I've seen a small part of what your lifestyle entails and how it changes you.'

She stepped up to him and he watched her with care. Who knew what she would do, but a part of him dared her to defy him as well. Knowing she sought a reaction, he schooled all expression from his face.

'This control freak is not the man I fell in love with.'

He almost stumbled back with the impact of those words. His heart squeezed and he struggled to maintain his cool composure. Struggled hard. Not something he was used to. Nothing about Kiri was what he was used to.

'I need control.' The words seemed almost torn from him and she stopped, as if arrested by the expression on his face.

Some nuance he hadn't intended had captured her attention, cut through her distress, sharpened her instincts. 'Why do you need control?'

He walked past her towards the sofa she'd slept on earlier. Unconsciously ran his fingers over the cushion she had rested her head on. As if touching this meant he touched her. Seeking comfort?

'How do you find my brother?'

Her lovely brows drew together. He imagined she thought this random. She shook her head. 'I'd look for Marla?' Shook it again. 'I don't want *to* talk about Theros.'

'I wait.'

She looked about the room as if seeking inspiration and finally shrugged. 'He seems nice.' She thought for a moment, he saw when the suspicion began to form in her mind. 'Is there something wrong with Theros?'

He closed his eyes and then opened them again. 'Did you know that Mikey's brother — Chris — woke up? He'll be fine. How do you feel about that?'

'You are random.'

He smiled. As he thought. Seemed he did have some insight into the way her mind worked. 'So it appears.'

'About Mikey? Relieved. I'm glad.' She sat down beside him as he stared straight ahead. She said nothing and the silence stretched between them.

Finally, he began to speak. 'There was an accident when we were children. Theros almost drowned in an ocean pool. I managed to resuscitate him but not fast or well enough. He is a child in a man's body because of me.'

'No. Stefanos, *no*,' she said again with more force. 'That is not your fault.'

He ignored that. Shrugged. Felt the guilt. Shame. Loss of control. 'I need control to ensure everyone stays safe.'

'How old were you?' She asked slowly, her eyes holding his with the oddest expression.

'Eight. He was six and I eight.'

Chapter 34: Kiri

'Eight years old?' Kiri's stomach dropped and she wanted to take his head in her hands and kiss him for the years of pain and self-flagellation she could now see he had been determined to endure. Had probably been *encouraged* to endure, if she'd read his father right. But she needed to speak carefully if he was ever to have peace. 'And you resuscitated your drowned brother?'

He flexed his shoulders. 'Not quickly enough to prevent damage.'

'You resuscitated your drowned brother, by yourself, so that he breathed again?'

'Yes.'

She saw him blink. Consider. Finally use his powerful brain to think about himself. He closed his eyes. Very slightly, he sagged.

She persisted. 'Would you have blamed Mikey if he had done the same?' Her heart cracked for him. Poor young boy Stefano.

His eyes flew open. He sat straighter. 'Of course not.'

She stared at him, but he refused to meet her determined gaze with his own. She lowered her voice but knew he heard every word. 'Then perhaps it is time to forgive yourself.'

He looked at her. Really looked. And she saw the man she fell in love with lurking in there. 'I fear I am destined to hurt the ones I love.'

She nodded and took his hand, stroked the strong fingers that had held her through memorable nights, felt his pain and rested his fingers against her heart. She understood him so much more.

'And that is the dilemma. Perhaps it's time to let go of that which can't be changed. Perhaps consider that happiness doesn't need perfection. Theros seems very happy. Marla seems happy.'

'He *is* happy when he isn't in trouble with me.' Seemed he could acknowledge that if he allowed himself to consider it.

She put his hand back down and moved hers away. 'Then let it go. You can't control everything.'

'Just forget? This guilt is like a blanket made of lead. It's been around my shoulders for as long as I can remember.' He squeezed his forehead. 'I wish I could just drop it.'

The grandmother clock began to chime and neither of them spoke as the toll rang out until midnight was proclaimed.

Suddenly Kiri realized the day she had dreaded was here. Her baby's arrival date that would never come. But, despite his presence, Stefano wasn't with her for that.

She stood up. She felt so tired. And there was so much to think about. Tonight she was going to try and do the same thing she'd told Stefano to do, because she'd promised herself that when this day came she would let go.

'Please leave. I'm tired and I can't think any more.'

She knew he could sense her withdrawal, so she was surprised when he asked, 'What if I don't want to go?'

Kiri turned her back on him, because she didn't have any reserves left to fight. 'I can't help that,' she said. And she walked away.

After an emotional discussion with her pillow Kiri slept fitfully. She was woken by Elise with coffee and croissants and a warning that soon the stylist would arrive to prepare her for a day of official functions.

Every time her mind wandered to the significance of the date she pushed it away.

The really bad news came with her breakfast. She must travel with Crown Prince Paulo in the official convoy.

She sipped her tea pensively. What the heck could she talk about? Or maybe you didn't talk to the Crown Prince — though an hour of disapproving silence would be like water torture.

By the time she was handed into the official car she was feeling surer than ever that she wasn't cut out for this life. And the royal scrutiny was such that she couldn't tell if he was satisfied with her appearance or not.

'Good morning, Dr Fender.'

'Good morning, Prince Paulo.' She slid past the footman holding the door and into the car.

'Did you sleep well?'

Apparently he did talk, and Kiri felt herself relax slightly. She usually did after a big cry. 'It was a different sleep than on the ship.'

'Of course.'

He transferred his attention to the cobbled streets of the castle forecourt as they began their journey and Kiri sighed. That was that, then. How had she ended up in a royal car with an autocratic old despot?

to

'If you don't mind me asking, why am I with you today, Prince Paulo?'

The Prince turned back her. 'Because Stefano is not. Too often he neglects his royal duties for his passion with surgery.' He glanced back out of the window. 'And see where that gets him.'

Kiri's sense of fairness disputed that. Couldn't he see the good Stefano did? The depth of care and kindness his son showed his patients was admirable, even if that kindness didn't extend to *her* at the present time.

Kiri narrowed her eyes on the back of the Prince's turned head. 'Your son saves lives. Has there not been a physician in your family since the first Mykonides?'

That swung his head. Now he was every inch the monarch. His bristled white brows soared, his eyes narrowed, and in that moment she saw the dark eyes of his son at their most arctic. 'Who are you to presume to tell me my own history?'

But strangely Kiri wasn't afraid or uncomfortable. It was as if a calm voice whispered in her ear to let him bluster.

She should say *she* was the woman pretending to be engaged to his son to help the family's good name. But she didn't need this man as her enemy. 'My apologies, Your Highness.'

But they both knew she wasn't cowed by him, and she wondered if she could detect just a glimpse of approval in his eyes.

In a more conciliatory tone she went on, 'I'm saying his skills as a surgeon are a gift.'

The Prince shrugged and allowed himself to stop pretending he was enraged. 'So they say.' He turned to look out of the window and she heard him mutter, 'He should be more of a prince.'

Kiri turned to her own window as they began their spiral descent of the mountain. 'He could hardly be more.'

She heard the indrawn breath of the old man but she couldn't regret it. What could he do? Put her out of the car. Well, yes please, she was happy with that idea.

'So you champion a man who leaves you pregnant in another country?'

It seemed the old man had rallied.

They faced each other like circling dogs. 'Circumstances were not kind to us.'

'If he has any of me in him he will not be kind to you either.' He glared at her, and then slowly his gaze softened. 'You remind me of someone I knew long ago. She too was fearless.' He laughed without amusement. 'And stubborn. This may not turn out badly yet.'

Kiri had nothing to say to that. Now she felt less sure of herself and wondered what had possessed her to take him on.

The drive through the olive groves passed silently and Kiri chewed on her lip as she worried what would be asked of her today.

Eventually the Prince roused himself from whatever had kept him in pensive silence. 'I think you should address the women. The patronesses. It is a gynecological ward we are opening. Thank them for their donations which have helped create the facility and they will be happy.'

Her worst nightmare. What should she say? 'Surely they would prefer your address to mine?'

'Ha! You are a woman.' He turned away. 'I have decided.'

Typical. Like father, like son, she thought with an unhappy sigh.

As Kiri came to the end of her speech — more of a lecture on meeting the health needs all women deserved — she added an informal thank you to the patronesses, and Prince Paulo seemed happy enough. It had proved less of a trial than she had anticipated. But it had been stressful, and underneath she seethed.

She'd had an epiphany. Here she was for these women, and today of all days Stefano, of course, was not here for *her*.

Kiri estimated there were about fifty well-dressed women, most of them around her age. With women's health so important she'd spoken from the heart, because that way at least she could be happy with her message.

Until she asked for questions and of course the most difficult one surfaced.

Kiri looked at the woman and something warned her. Despite her designer clothes, her coiffed hair, she had sad, sad eyes, and Kiri knew this woman struggled in a dark place too.

The woman moistened her lips and Kiri leaned forward slightly to hear. 'Are you afraid of miscarrying again?'

Kiri winced internally but here she was a professional. Tense but open. 'Yes. But as a doctor I remind myself that one miscarriage, or even two miscarriages, does not mean I am more at risk. Yes, it crosses my mind, but I have to trust in the future.'

The woman smiled gently, closed her eyes and nodded. Then she whispered, 'I lost my baby last month.'

Kiri's eyes stung as she stepped down off the little podium. The others parted to let her through, and the two women embraced. Quietly but unashamedly, so it carried to everyone in the room, Kiri said, 'Our baby would have been due today.'

When they drew apart and smiled mistily at each other, Kiri knew she had found a friend, and for the first time she thought perhaps there *were* things she could achieve here if she and Stefano ever worked it out. But at this moment that seemed very unlikely. And the waste made her angrier.

Out of the corner of her eye she saw Prince Paulo gesture to the Mayor to conclude the event, and she mentally prepared herself for the trip back in the Prince's company.

Bruno directed her to the podium again and then turned to the audience. 'Thank you so much, Dr Fender, for your sincerity. We are all deeply appreciative of your presence today.'

Kiri stepped back, the crowd began to disperse, and she gathered her emotions and control. Just.

Until she saw Stefano arrive and cross to his father. She narrowed her eyes. *Great timing,* she thought, *when it's too late to support me but in time to judge me.* Her anger stepped up another notch.

Of all days she had had to do this and he didn't even know.

Stefano spoke briefly to his father and she saw Prince Paulo pat his son's shoulder in an unusual gesture of affection. He nodded in her direction, and with his entourage cordially turned away.

Stefano crossed to her side. He seemed bemused. 'My father said you did well. That the women liked you. Congratulations.'

Something snapped inside her. 'How generous of you, Highness. My thanks for your kind words.'

She saw he didn't miss the sarcasm and was glad. How dared he? She "did well?" So magnanimous of him.

Was she supposed to be thrilled at his approval? And what if she hadn't done well, would he have been here to support her?

His gaze narrowed. 'You're angry? With me?'

'How perceptive you are. Do you know what I spoke about; what I told them?'

He shook his head warily, and she could feel emotion bubbling to the surface when she wanted to remain ice-cold. Angry tears stung her eyes and she turned away from him, because the words wouldn't come. She wanted them to spill out, hurt him as they hurt her, but she couldn't make her mouth work.

Chapter 35: Stefano

Stefano followed her as she walked blindly along the corridor back towards the entrance, and once he steered her gently when she would have taken a wrong turn.

He didn't know what to do. He could see that Kiri seethed with emotion. Had he pushed her too far by expecting her to do this today? But he'd had to operate. He reminded himself that she hadn't been trained for official occasions as he had, and yet every time he asked something of her, she responded magnificently. But at what cost?

She swept out of the hospital and he kept pace, nodding at those he passed as if it was his decision to continue this headlong race she had begun.

She stopped. At his car. Spun to face him. The look in her eyes made him step back.

'Do you know what you asked of me today?'

He didn't want to know right here, right now, because it was not going to be pretty. He opened her door. 'Please, first sit.'

She opened and shut her mouth, and with relief he saw she would do as he asked. When he slid behind the wheel her emotion was like a wall between them and he put up his hand as if to touch it.

'Can I ask you to wait a few more minutes? For the privacy you deserve, not for me. I wish to give you my undivided attention.'

Again, she nodded, and he started the car and drove along the road until he came to a lay-by that overlooked the olive groves. He turned the engine off and faced her. Drew a breath and prepared for an avalanche. He got it.

'Since yesterday morning my life has not been my own.'

Finally the words spilled, and he bowed his head and took them. Not wincing, at least for himself, he listened. He wanted to understand.

'You have accused me of many things, all of them incorrect, and you have constantly thrown me into situations that were beyond my control.' She drew another breath.

He knew it was true. Last night, when he'd finally stopped thinking about himself, he had begun to realize just what he had put her through. And yet still she had been there for him. The more he had considered it, the more he'd been able to see the many ways in which he had failed her.

He deserved every accusation for the mistakes he'd made. For his need to maintain control over his life, a need he could not let go of. He wanted to say he was sorry for whatever he'd done, to hold her, comfort her. But the wall between them kept him back.

'Can you tell me what happened in there?'

She jabbed her finger towards his head. 'Can *you* tell me what happens in *there?* In your closely guarded mind that simply refuses to open to me. To trust.' She shook her head with frustration. 'You expect so little from me—'

'No.'

'Yes,' Kiri insisted. 'You would rather think I am a woman who will fail you than a woman who can succeed. I can succeed at anything.' Her eyes shone with held back tears. 'And I can succeed without you, Stefano.'

'You have more than proved that.' He lifted his chin, aching to touch her, comfort her. 'Not once have you failed me. It is the other way round.'

Her eyes glittered still. 'I know. Why is that?'

He had no answer. He watched her shudder against the door as she leaned as far away as possible from him. His hand clenched uselessly, because at this moment he couldn't mistake her aversion to his touch.

'Today I was there for those women in a way you have never been for me.' Her profile lit by the sunshine outside as she held some distant landmark in her gaze. 'And it came home to me just how much you have let me down. Such a waste when we could have been so good together. And, yes, it makes me very angry.'

She turned, pointed an accusing finger at him, and glared. 'I gave more than I thought I would have to. Again, without your support. In the last few days I have been forced to publicly expose my pain again and again, and you know what?' Her determined chin dropped, her eyes left his and she clasped her hands. 'I can't do it anymore.'

For the first time he could see her perspective. She was right, and he hastened to reassure her. 'I won't ask it of you.'

She turned towards him and he saw the tears in her eyes, could feel her hurt in his own chest. She straightened her shoulders. As always, her strength astounded him. He could hear the control she clung to in her voice. 'You've missed the whole point of what I needed from you. Especially today.'

The words captured him. It was there. Something in her voice... 'Why today?'

She didn't answer that immediately and he almost missed the significance. Again.

'Because it's heartbreaking to lose a baby. And today should have been about life, not loss.'

'Today?' The full import of what she was saying smashed into his brain like a ship into rocks. Along with the anguish in her voice. Today?

He read the confirmation on Kiri's face and realized he truly did deserve to lose not only his child but this woman. And just when he'd come to understand how much he needed her in his life. That he didn't ever want to lose her. Couldn't lose her.

He was so afraid that he had finally, completely, driven her away.

Stefano knew it was time to battle his own demons. To risk everything. Because if he didn't he would lose the best thing that had ever happened to him.

He reached for her, and to his shuddering relief this time she didn't pull away. He slid his finger under her chin and gently turned her to him, so he could cradle her face in his hands, stare into her beautiful eyes. 'I am so, so sorry I was not there.'

He saw the reflection of his own sense of loss for what they'd had between them and ached to ease her pain.

'I am sorry,' he said again, his poor Kiri, hurting so badly because today was to be the birth of their baby. He held her now. He needed to think of her not himself. Why did he always do and say the wrong thing around this woman? 'What I have done to you is unforgivable.' He reflected over the last twenty-four hours and winced. His voice gentle for her but inside he was bitter at his own stupidity. 'My anger at the public scrutiny didn't take into account the cost to you.'

Mental screenshots flickered past like a horror film. The way he had dragged her to the palace, thrust his mother's ring on her finger, installed her in his mother's isolated rooms with barely an explanation. Left her alone to suffer while he'd worried more about reputation.

To make matters a hundred times worse he had then forced her to attend a ceremonial function that very night, most probably because he had truly expected her to fail. Then he would have been able to tell himself it would never work.

Poor, poor Kiri, who didn't deserve his idiocy but whom he hoped would forgive.

He heard the rasp as she drew in her breath. Watched her blink away the tears that glittered on her lashes as she raised her head. He could not read the expression. He had lost her.

'I was a monster to you.' His voice cracked and his chest hurt. He didn't deserve her.

'Yes, you were.' But then touched his face. 'All that and more.' She shifted her head back a little, so she could focus. 'Why?'

He had nothing left to give her but the truth. 'Because I was afraid.'

'Of me?'

Of the loss. 'Of course of you. Of what you meant to me.' He ran his hands through his hair and let himself voice the words. His true fear. 'Of losing control of my life.'

'Explain.'

Was she giving him a chance? This lifeline? He must grab and hold onto this second chance. This was too important to him not to. So let him make this progression in his thoughts. I don't like him giving in so easily, not after she's given him some home.

'This life is a lot to ask of you. And yet you have risen again and again at each challenge. I should have believed more in you and more in us. And yet I fear it is too late.'

She said again. 'What are you talking about?'

'Already I have hurt you in so many ways because of my fears. I will take you back to the mainland this afternoon.'

'You still don't get it. I don't want to go. You've been horrible, but I'll survive.'

His hand lifted and one finger stroked her silken cheek. 'I know you will survive. You are magnificent. Last night you rose and faced them all as if you had been born to stand head and shoulders above the world.' He was so proud of her, and ashamed of being the man who had subjected her to that. 'No thanks to me.'

She went on in her calm voice. 'And today I was there for those women in a way you have never been for me. It came home to me just how much you have let me down. And, yes, it makes me very angry.'

Her lips tilted, teased him, and his fear eased a little that she could still smile his way.

'Some things I *can* thank you for. You rescued me from the press at the dock.'

'Pah.' He snapped his fingers. 'That is nothing. I should not have left you. Well before that I was not there when you needed me the most.'

Stefano leant across and gathered her in, felt her slight weight against him. 'I wish I had protected you from the world from the start.' He tilted his head down to see her. 'But I am now, for she who is my partner, my equal, we are a team of two to take on the world.'

'At last. And you are here now,' she said.

Finally, he was truly beginning to understand the wonder that was his Kiri. It had taken him too long to realize that was his mission. He drew her even closer. 'Is it true that our baby was to have been born today?'

She nodded her head against him. Whispered, 'Yes,' and his heart contracted.

He moistened his lips, prayed she would hear the truth in his words, and finally said what he should have said when he'd first found out that they had made a baby together. 'I am so sorry I was not there with you when our child slipped away from us.'

Her eyes shadowed as she returned to her most painful memory, allowed him to see the pain and the loss, as if through a small window to how it had been. She acknowledged his right to see, and he realized that was the greatest gift she had given him yet.

'It was night and I was alone.' Kiri pressed her lips together to stop their wobble.

He closed his eyes and breathed deeply, more ashamed than he had ever been in all his life. 'My poor, poor love. I wish I could have held you and shared your grief. I should have been there. Let me share it now.' He squeezed her to him as he felt the dampness of his own eyes. 'Please.'

Kiri turned her face into his chest and he stroked her hair and encouraged her to purge that night in the hospital. He did not expect the sawing wound of pain her words would create.

'I was alone. The room was dark and metallic and the loneliest place in the world when the pains increased.'

He kissed her. Quiet. Aching as she talked.

'Suddenly blood gushed so fast the nurse rushed off and then I was in Theatre.' She whispered into the silence and he was there with her, in that hospital, by her side as he should have been.

'I knew that when I woke up from the anesthetic it would be gone. Not just our baby, but any link to you.'

'My darling Kiri. I'm so sorry.'

And then the tears came, great gulping sobs, tearing both their hearts, until finally he could share as he wrapped her in his arms. Arms that he should have offered so many lonely nights ago.

And at last, after far too long, the final healing could begin.

Stefano held her tightly against him, gathering her shudders of grief as he pulled her closer, inhaling the scent of her hair, stroking her over and over again with all the tenderness he had in him. He had never felt as close to anyone in his whole life as he did to this woman at this moment. Had never allowed himself to do so in case he lost himself. But now he wanted to be lost.

Lost with her.

Random flashes of his past with Kiri rolled through his mind.

The first time he'd seen her, like a ray of sunshine in his day, radiant, confident, joyous. A heroine on her quest to help mankind.

The first time he'd held her hand and sensed there was something between them that defied description yet was instantly recognizable — something he would never forget despite all the obstacles fate had thrown up against them.

And that magical week when she had opened her home, her arms, and her heart just for him. Stefano the man — not Stefano the Prince. Even when he'd been away, recovering, she'd been like a shadow behind him that refused to be forgotten.

He would make it up to her. He would make it all up to her. He just hoped she felt the same about him, because now that he had her back in his arms he didn't think he could let her go. Ever.

Slowly her weeping turned to hiccups and her flood of tears to a trickle. He mopped her face and hugged her again and kissed her damp mouth gently. He wanted to repeat his apology, but he was afraid she would weep all over again.

But Kiri was made of sterner stuff than that. One last sniff, the hijacking of his handkerchief, and she wiped her eyes and blew her nose resolutely. 'I'm sorry.'

'As am I.'

'That was torrential. Thank you for letting me soak your shirt.'

The knot in his stomach loosened. 'You are very welcome.'

She sniffed again and smiled, with a tiny wobble still in evidence. 'Thank you, anyway. I think I needed that.'

In wonder, he watched the old Kiri re-emerge and sat back on his side of the car with bemusement and wonder. Relief expanded in his chest as he realized she had already begun to forgive him. Now all he had to do was forgive himself.

Chapter 36: Kiri

Kiri screwed up the handkerchief after one last trumpeting blow. If he still fancied her after this then there was hope for them yet. But that thought and all it involved filled her with terrifying doubt all over again.

There was this Stefano, the man she loved – and who she now believed loved her, and then there was the other. Stefano the Prince.

'Thank you for listening, and for being here now.' She glanced around at the grove of olives across the road. They were sitting in a sports car on an island in the Med. 'But perhaps we should talk of something else.'

He didn't move.

'Or head back to the castle?'

It was as if he couldn't hear her. The way his gaze moved across her face made her cheeks burn. His grey eyes were softer than she'd ever seen them, and he kissed her fingers and brushed her cheek with a gesture of infinite tenderness. More heat to her red face, and she looked away, embarrassed, suddenly remembering again that this man was a prince and she'd sobbed all over him.

'How was I so fortunate as to find you?' He shook his head in wonder, and as if unable to help himself, reached and took her hand.

They both gazed down at the ring he'd insisted she wear. The huge square diamond flashed with reflected light even when there didn't seem to be any beams to catch. His mother's. It wasn't hers. Not really.

He leaned forward and spoke very slowly and gently. 'So, my question is this. To the world we are already engaged, but the man who demanded this did not deserve you.'

He stroked the ring on her finger and drew it off. To her dismay, she felt bereft. It had come to this. Where they faced the truth. She drew in a breath and steadied herself for the end.

He raised her hand to his lips and caressed her knuckles with his mouth. 'May I start again?'

She blinked, not sure what he meant. A crazy, stuttering hope like a flame caught in a cross breeze tossed her into confusion. Start again? Where? With what?

Stefano searched her face. She tried to hide her confusion, her stupid hope, and her misgivings. He saw her turmoil, she knew he did.

He drew a deeper breath. 'Do you know that I love you?'

Hope flared and she opened her mouth and closed it. Then finally she said, 'No.'

She saw his dismay as she shook her head. 'I love you and wish to spend my life with you. To respect and honor you. But only if this is what you want, too.'

He knew she had seen what living here with him would mean and chosen him anyway. The enormous commitment. The bravery of his Kiri.

'Will you share my life with me, do me the honor of becoming my wife? That is the most important.'

She nodded. 'I will.'

'And second to that, will you be my princess when needed? Wear this ring with all it entails?'

She looked down at the ring in his hand. Remembered the weight of it. The rules and etiquette, royal crises and formal functions, the responsibilities of a title. Could she?

But their work at the hospital would keep them busy and grounded. She thought of the women, of the first of many friends she could make, of those she could help. The children recovering from tragic injuries without their families.

Then Kiri imagined a life never seeing Stefano again, losing her unfulfilled dream of dark-haired arrogant little boys like Stefano and tiny little girls in pink tulle, and there was no contest.

She would not be alone. She would have Stefano the person. Not just the heir to the throne. Her doctor, teacher, humanitarian. Her brilliant, loving, gorgeous man. Stefano.

She leaned across and kissed him fully on the lips. 'I love you. Will always love you.'

'But?' he asked, seeing that hint of hesitancy in her eyes.

'The princess part does fill me with some trepidation.'

He kissed her back. 'I understand, my love. I vow to share with you, to help you, guide you, be there for you because together we can achieve great things. We are two halves of the whole. Doing our roles together.'

This was what she truly wanted. Finally, he understood what she needed. Them. Together. 'Two halves of whole,' she whispered.

He slid the ring back on her finger with immense satisfaction. Surprisingly the weight of it felt good.

Stefano stroked her hand and smiled. 'Already I feel the weight of the coming years grow lighter. I will never let you down again.'

'You hope,' she said, 'because I'll make you sorry.'

Her prince said softly, 'I cannot wait.'

Chapter 37: Kiri

Kiri's brother Nick arrived to find out just what was happening to his sister. Instead, he accepted an invitation to an engagement party.

There was to be a magnificent celebration for the engagement of Prince Stefano Mykonides and his bride-to-be, Dr Kristina Karine Fender, and the whole island was invited.

Open-sided marquees provided for the guests to wander through, delicacies and drink, barbecues, and samples of strange Australian damper loaves and lemon meringue pies, Kiri's special dessert. The night sang, music lifted to the skies from short cameos from the world's greatest musicians and quirky alternatives like Kiri's favorite Australian country band, flown over at the last minute.

As a gift and gesture of acknowledgment, Stefano had set up a huge screen — a never-ending light show depicting the glory of his betrothed's homeland. From harbor to Outback, it showed soaring scenery, a bird's-eye view circumnavigating the whole coastline and across the continent. From Barrier Reef to Uluru, the screen breathed life into a continent thousands of miles away, so that his people understood that he was a part of that world as his bride was now a part of theirs.

And through it all Kiri and Stefano walked among the villagers, the townsfolk, their hospital colleagues, and the castle staff, shaking hands, smiling at each other and at the world. For Kiri, the magnitude of the spectacle had started as a challenge but then she'd met people she knew. Dr Herore and her husband. Rosa's family. Sheba and the new baby. Elise had brought her son and to Kiri's surprise, Jerome. Stefano had whispered that Elise had asked for his thoughts on adoption.

Kiri began to enjoy meeting the hundreds of people they spoke to, all eager to wish them well and ask about the wedding. Kiri's brother Nick shook his head repeatedly at his little sister's surprise rise to fame.

Wilhelm and Miko from the ship were there and, audaciously, Miko kissed Kiri's hand right in front of her fiancé. Kiri laughed and Stefano growled good-naturedly about it being his last chance to do so.

But finally, well after midnight, the spectacle was over and Stefano kissed her as soon as they were through the door of their apartments. He swept her up in his arms and carried her through to her bedroom. 'I have been waiting to do this all night.'

It felt so good to have his arms around her and finally she could allow the world to disappear. She leaned across and kissed him softly on the lips. 'Thank you for the party. The Aussie touches. Such an extravaganza, but this is enough for me.'

Epilogue

Six months later, in the red silk-lined formal throne room of the palace, arranged in front of the huge gold fireplace and the soaring portraits of the current ruler and his late princess, in the presence of Prince Paulo, Prince Theros and his wife Princess Marla, a dozen dignitaries, and the bride's four siblings and their partners, a civil ceremony of marriage was carried out by His Excellency the Mayor, Bruno Valinari.

Kiri, dressed in coral colored Dior, sat straight-backed, her hands folded demurely in her lap, as she listened to the long legal discourse required before Stefano could legally make her his princess.

Eventually the moment arrived, and without hesitation his voice decreed his intention. 'I pledge my life and legally bind myself to Kristina Karine Fender. My Princess.' And then softly, with joy and belief as he met her eyes, 'My Kiri.'

The Mayor said, 'For ever?'

'I will.'

Her eyes stung but she sucked in a deep breath and fought the tears hard. She didn't think princesses were allowed to cry. She'd meant to ask Elise.

Then it was her turn and she listened, minute after minute, to the legal jargon mixed with advice in the way of royal wedding ceremonies for the last five hundred years on this sovereign island discovered by pirates and ruled by physicians.

The longer the discourse went on the more nervous she became. Her heart began to pound. She would miss her cue, would stumble, would open her mouth and no sound would come out.

Suddenly she became conscious that tomorrow, in the cathedral, it would be a thousand times worse, with millions upon millions of television viewers. What if her words got stuck?

The Mayor's words seemed to join together in her ears, so she couldn't tell where one began and the other ended, and the lump in her throat grew so large she could barely breathe. Her mouth dried and she began to shake as a surge of adrenaline coursed through her body and made her want to stand up and run.

At last now she understood those movies where the bride bolted.

Then gradually, as if directed by a hand other than her own, she lifted her eyes to the portrait of Stefano's mother, who seemed to glow down of them from above the gold fireplace. The beautiful woman in the gilt frame smiled. *My love to you both.* The words were as clear as if she were sitting beside the mother-in-law she would never meet.

See only one person or the occasion will overwhelm you.

Kiri felt the knot that had tied her tongue ease and drift away as if it had never been. *Look, speak, and smile at one person and you will be in control of the room.* That was easy and closed her eyes. There was only one person.

When she opened her eyes, the room had narrowed to the one person who mattered — the man she loved with all her heart and who would stand beside her anywhere. Joined to Stefano, she would never be afraid again.

All nervousness fled and she lifted her chin.

The moment appeared, and she was so very ready. 'I pledge my life to you, Stefano Adolphi Phillipe Augustus Mykonides.' She smiled. 'My Stefano.'

The Mayor said, 'For ever?'

'I will.'

And they were wed.

When they stepped out onto the balcony of the palace the square below had filled with Stefano's people — her people now — and the roar of the crowd swelled like the roar of a train, building in intensity and promising to carry her into a new life and new experiences.

Stefano turned her to him and she lifted her face for their first kiss as man and wife. As his lips touched hers the roar of the crowd doubled until they broke apart and smiled at their world.

On the morning of their cathedral wedding, Stefano and Kiri lay entwined, heavily asleep, smiles on their faces and hands clasped.

Elise didn't want to wake them, so she sent Jerome.

'Wake up!'

The young boy had a part to play today and he wanted to get started.

Four hours later in the bride's chambers it was time to leave for the cathedral. It was good to have Nick's hand to stop her trembling, but Kiri could see that today it seemed her big brother was the more nervous one.

Nick had told her that yesterday he'd thought she would faint from fright. He had been worried his little sister had chosen far too public a road for herself. But today she was a new woman, and she could see the look of love and awe on his face and it gave her even more confidence.

Her dress had been created by the principal of a famous Parisian couture house, with lace inserts from its high neck to under her bodice, sewn with a thousand crystals and the fall of a thousand seated pearls. The train had her six attendants scurrying, and made Nick shake his head in male confusion.

And the veil... Her mother-in-law's own veil, a thousand hours of stitching and twenty yards long, it was so thin and insubstantial it was like looking through a cobweb.

Nick scratched his chin. 'I have no idea how they're going to get this dress into the car.'

Kiri shrugged and twitched her sleeve straight. 'Don't worry. They'll have an expert do it. And it's a very long car.' Already she had learnt.

Her brother raised his brows, threw back his head and laughed.

'What?'

Nick glanced at the open door held by a liveried footman and then back at his radiant sister. 'You've changed.'

She lifted her head. 'I've accepted and I'm blessed.'

She would take everything in her stride. One thing at a time. Because at the end of the day would be Stefano.

'I'm Stefano's wife. I'm going to be a very good one. And I'm not going to worry about the minutiae or I'll go insane.'

They did get the dress into the Rolls Royce. Just. With a hundred perfect folds so that it would leave the car as beautiful as it had gone in.

The streets were lined with flag-waving residents as Kiri and Nick drove slowly towards the cathedral. They passed huge screens set up on walls to televise the wedding to those outside. Two cars behind, her six attendants followed. Her own three sisters, three small royal flower girls and one little pageboy, smiling so hard the scars on his face shone white in the sunlight.

Jerome's was the face of joy projected around the world which encompassed the celebration for the people in the streets.

Finally their favorite prince had wed. They loved their new princess, and they were all invited.

Stefano arrived at the cathedral first, and the crowd roared their approval that he had shunned protocol and chosen to arrive first and wait for his commoner wife. He turned, waved, and entered the building.

Theros accompanied him nervously down the long red carpet to the marble altar at the front. Every red velvet seat was taken. Every foot of space was jammed with bodies and cameras.

Theros kept patting his pocket, where the rings sat. He and Marla had eloped to avoid this very spectacle. This was frighteningly huge but for his brother he would brave the world.

Nervous afterwards, and frightened of the cathedral, he was diffident about following his brother, but his own bride had been so sure he could do it and he was determined he would.

Stefano recognized his brother's distress. 'Thank you for standing by me, Theros.' He lowered his head and spoke quietly, so the microphones wouldn't pick it up. 'I wanted to marry here. Mama is here, and I want her to meet my new princess.'

Then the music started, played by the minstrels in the gallery on golden horns, a serenade on the bride's arrival. Stefano felt his heart trip. So much he had asked of a woman not born to this, and to every new challenge she had risen, teaching him so much about true inner strength. So brave was his bride, and he could not wait for her to stand here beside him and before God.

Then she was at the door, on the arm of his new brother-in-law.

She was a vision. An angel in white with her head held high. Through the fine mist of her veil her eyes searched, found his, stayed fixed and the music swelled. But it was no match for the swelling in his heart as the woman of his dreams walked slowly towards him. Everything else faded. There was just this woman, fearlessly announcing to the world that she would love him forever.

As he would love her.

www.ingramcontent.com/pod-product-compliance
Lightning Source LLC
Chambersburg PA
CBHW020517120726
47904CB00003B/863